The Younger

Brother

VIVIAN SINCLAIR

Copyright

This book is a work of fiction. Names, characters, and incidents either are the product of the author's imagination or are used fictitiously. Any resemblance to actual persons, living or dead, or events is entirely coincidental.

Cover design: Vivian Sinclair

Cover illustrations credit:
> © Perseomedusa | Dreamstime.com
> © Derrick Neill | Dreamstime.com

ISBN: 9781793456847

To find out about new releases and about other books written by Vivian Sinclair visit her website at VivianSinclairBooks.com or follow her on the Author page at Amazon, Facebook at Vivian Sinclair Books, or on GoodReads.com

Old West Wyoming - western historical fiction
Book 1 - A Western Christmas
Book 2 - The Train To Laramie
Book 3 - The Last Stagecoach

Tales Of Old Wyoming – western historical fiction
Book 1 – The Younger Brother
Book 2 – A Stranger In Town
Book 3 – Going West
Book 4 – The Revenge

Starting Over in Wyoming - western contemporary fiction
Book 1 – Riding Alone
Book 2 – The Old Homestead
Book 3 – On The Hunt

Maitland Legacy, A Family Saga - western contemporary fiction
Book 1 – Lost In Wyoming – Lance's story
Book 2 – Moon Over Laramie – Tristan's story
Book 3 – Christmas In Cheyenne – Raul's story

Wyoming Christmas – western contemporary fiction
Book 1 – Footprints In The Snow – Tom's story
Book 2 – A Visitor For Christmas – Brianna's story

Book 3 – Trapped On The Mountain – Chris' story

Summer Days In Wyoming - western contemporary fiction
Book 1 – A Ride In The Afternoon
Book 2 – Fire At Midnight
Book 3 – Misty Meadows At Dawn

Tales of Old Wyoming - western historical fiction
Book 1 – A Stranger In Town
Book 2 – Going West
Book 3 – The Younger Brother

Seattle Rain series - women's fiction novels
Book 1 - A Walk In The Rain
Book 2 – Rain, Again!
Book 3 – After The Rain

Virginia Lovers - contemporary romance:
Book 1 – Alexandra's Garden
Book 2 – Ariel's Summer Vacation
Book 3 – Lulu's Christmas Wish

A Guest At The Ranch – western contemporary romance

Storm In A Glass Of Water – a small town story

CHAPTER 1

Laramie, Wyoming Territory, Summer of 1888

The train had just left Cheyenne twenty minutes ago and had about two more hours until it arrived in Laramie. The passengers were nodding off, lulled to sleep by the rhythmic movement of the carriage and the clicking noise of the wheels on tracks.

The young man sitting near the window was looking outside at the markers in the landscape rapidly passing by, boulders and scraggly bushes left behind in the blink of an eye. What a marvelous invention the train was, he thought. He could have lived all his life on the farm in Kansas and never known what was in the world out there. For a moment, the memory of his parents darkened his blue eyes with pain. In a matter of days, both had been taken away from the living by typhus. However, he was a cheerful fellow and tried not to dwell too long on unhappy memories. He tried to have hope for the future.

On the bench in front of him, the older lady with lots of flowers and cherries on her hat smiled at him. "Are you going west young man?" It was a pointless question because he was already on a train in a western territory.

He returned her smile. "Yes, ma'am. I'm going to Laramie to meet my brother."

"I think he'll appreciate that you left the east coast to visit him."

His eyes reflected worry for a moment. "I'm from Kansas, not from the east, and my brother doesn't know I'm coming. He was the eldest and he left home twenty years ago. I'm the youngest of seven."

"You'll be a nice surprise for him." She leaned forward to impart a secret. "You and me both. My son doesn't know I'm coming either." And she giggled like a young girl.

The train stopped suddenly with a sharp screech of the wheels and before the passengers could understand what was going on, the door at one end of the carriage opened and a man entered. He had half his face covered by a dark bandanna and a gun in his hand.

"Take out all your valuables, money and jewelry, and hand them over."

A woman started to wail loudly and the robber shot near her feet. "I am warning you. Don't make me mad."

When the robber reached their bench, the young man threw in the robber's bag a small leather pouch with a few pennies in it. There went his lunch, but he was lucky to have hidden the three hundred dollars he had received after selling the farm.

"Your watch," the robber demanded.

"I don't have one," he answered opening his coat to show his shirt under it.

The robber huffed his displeasure and turned his attention to the older woman. He raised his hand to grab the locket she wore on a chain over her dress.

She covered it with her own hand, "I received it from my husband on our wedding day forty years ago."

"It's not gold anyway, let it go, lady," the young man said to her.

The woman opened her mouth to contradict him. Then she thought better of it and snapped her mouth shut.

The door at the other end of the carriage opened and another man entered. "US Marshal, drop your gun."

Fast as lightening, the robber grabbed the older woman and pulled her in front of him. "You drop the gun or I'll blow her brains out," he said threatening, holding his gun at her temple.

After a moment of hesitation, the marshal dropped his gun to the floor.

"Oh, she's fainting," the young man said, looking at the frightened woman intently. Instantly, she became a dead weight and slid down to the floor. The robber couldn't support all her weight upright and eased his hold on her.

In a fraction of a second, the marshal pulled out of his coat another gun and shot the robber. The young man grabbed the older woman's hand and pulled her back on the wooden seat, out of the line of fire.

Women started to cry, a child asked, "Mama, is the bad man dead?" and in all this chaos, the marshal reached the robber and checked him.

"He's not dead," he said disappointed, hefting the wounded man on his shoulder.

"Now you'll have to carry him all the way to the Territorial Prison in Laramie," another man said.

The lawman shrugged. "We'll have to carry them all. Two dead and this one wounded. They have to be identified before being buried." The wounded man produced a lugubrious moan. "The dead ones, not you. Although probably that will be your fate too. You knew that, once you started down this path," the lawman concluded.

He dropped the wounded man on an empty bench near the exit and expertly shackled his hands. Then he went outside the carriage on the small platform to signal the conductor to start the train.

"You saved my life… and Harold's locket," the older woman said to the young man with a wobbly smile. "I'm Edith Heller, nice meeting you."

"Pierce Monroe," he said smiling and showing two attractive dimples. He was not fazed at all by the dangerous situation that had threatened their lives just a few moments ago.

While other people retrieved their personal objects from the robber's bag, the older woman bent and grabbed the gun that the robber had dropped right under their seat. "Do you want his gun?" she asked the young man.

"No. I don't plan on killing anyone."

She shrugged and placed it in her reticule. "You might not have a choice. Like now for instance - it's his life or ours. Also it might act as a deterrent to discourage others to shoot at you."

When the train stopped in the Laramie station with a piercing whistle, there was a collective sigh of relief from the passengers.

The young man helped the older woman to exit the carriage and to step down on the platform. She arranged to have her trunk delivered to one of the boarding houses in town. Then she turned to the young man to say Good-bye. "You take care, you hear?" she said straightening his collar.

THE YOUNGER BROTHER

The gesture was so familiar and reminded him of his mother that he felt tears pooling at the corner of his eyes. He had to look away and coughed to mask the strong emotion that threatened to overcome him. He only nodded.

"Good," she said, patting his coat. "You stay out of trouble. I'll see you around." She turned and waving her hand at him, she made her way down the street.

Pierce Monroe decided to ask the young clerk who had directed the train's departure where the sheriff's office was. The last letter received from his brother Bill, about seven years ago, said that he was sheriff in this town. Pierce hoped that he was still here. If not, Pierce had plenty of time to look for Bill; like the rest of his life. He had no definite plans for the future.

He found the clerk outside the station trying to calm an agitated horse harnessed to a buggy. Pierce didn't know much about the rest of the world outside the farm where he had grown up, but he knew horses. This was a spirited gelding who expected to be ridden in the saddle and not to pull a buggy.

"Hey, I don't think he likes to be hitched up to the buggy," Pierce said.

The clerk looked back at him, still holding the bridle. "I know you. You arrived with the train from Cheyenne, didn't you?"

"You have good memory. It's true, I did," Pierce answered liking the young clerk, even if he knew nothing about handling horses. "How did you get such a high-spirited horse?"

The clerk let go of the bridle. "I'm Timmy and I work here at the station. I do most everything the stationmaster needs done." He looked at the horse resentful. "You won't believe how I got this contrary animal. His owner left the buggy and the horse in my care and got into a fight with a cowboy outside the… house of… anyhow he got himself killed. I asked the stationmaster what to do with his belongings and he said they are mine. The owner had no known family in town. He worked here and there and had won the buggy and the horse in a game of cards."

"That's quite a story," Pierce said marveling how

precarious life was and how unpredictable.

"The trouble is that I live in town with my Ma and I don't have time and money to spend on a horse, to feed him, and curry him. Ma has a placid mare and a wagon and that is all we need. This horse adds an extra cost that I can't afford." He measured Pierce with interest. "Say, don't you want to buy it? I'll give it to you cheap."

Pierce didn't answer. He extended his hand to the horse. The gelding stopped bobbing his head up and down and pulling at the harness. He twitched his ears and looked at Pierce with distrust, but without stepping back. Pierce touched his nostrils gently, slowly moving his hand, letting the animal sniff it.

"Be careful, he'll chomp off your fingers," Timmy warned him.

"Nah, he's cautious. He doesn't know what to expect of me," Pierce explained.

It looked like Pierce passed the test and the horse decided he could trust him so he butted Pierce playfully in the chest. Pierce ran his hands over the horse's flanks.

"He's well formed and he was not mistreated. There are no signs of abuse."

"I'm surprised. The owner called him Devil and said he needs a whip to teach him who's in charge," Timmy told him scratching his head. "I guess he didn't get to buy that whip before he was killed."

Pierce almost crossed himself. "That's not a good name for the horse. Angel would be better."

Timmy looked at him horrified. "Angel is a woman working at the saloon. How about you give me ten dollars for the buggy and the horse and you can think of a name latter." The young clerk was set on concluding this business.

"Look, it's worth much more than ten dollars. You could get at least fifty only for the horse and perhaps as much for the buggy," Pierce assured him in all honesty.

"If I go to the stables, Marty Rogers will give me exactly ten dollars, no more. He'll tell me a Banbury tale that the horse is deformed and the buggy needs repairs. I know he will," Timmy argued. "And you need a horse for whatever business you have in town. Unless you plan to leave town by train tomorrow and I know you didn't buy a ticket."

That was true. So, Pierce paid the ten dollars and left driving the buggy after Timmy gave him directions to the Sheriff's Office.

CHAPTER 2

The Sheriff's Office was a newer building not far from the train station. Or at least it looked recently painted. Pierce stopped his newly acquired buggy in front and vaulted down. He patted the horse's neck assuring him that as soon as he found his brother, his next priority would be to feed the horse.

Then, he looked at the door, straightened his coat, took a deep breath, and entered the office. There was only one other person inside. A man was sitting in the chair behind the desk, in a relaxed pose, reading a newspaper. He was perhaps a few years older than Pierce, but too young to be his brother Bill.

The man was absorbed in his reading, even laughing once or twice. Pierce looked at the pages discarded on the desk - 'The Baltimore Sun'. Why would a sheriff in Wyoming be interested in an East coast newspaper?

Pierce cleared his throat loudly.

"I heard you," the man said, regretfully folding

the paper and setting it aside for later. "And I know it's not an emergency."

"How do you know?" Pierce asked with curiosity.

The man grinned and leaned back in his chair to have a better look at Pierce. "You'd have burst in my office, pushing the door to the wall with enough force to shatter the glass, babbling your story. And even in such case, it is not always a real emergency. Now, what can I do for you?"

"I'm looking for the sheriff."

The man opened his arms. "You found him. Gabe McCarthy, at your service."

Pierce shuffled his feet. The letter from Bill was seven years old. Was it possible that Bill had moved on and Pierce had come on a wild goose chase? "I'm looking for Sheriff Monroe. Is he still sheriff here?"

McCarthy narrowed his eyes. "What business do you have with Sheriff Monroe?"

"I'm his brother. Pierce Monroe from Kansas. Our parents died of typhus and I sold the farm and…"

"And you didn't know what to do with yourself,"

McCarthy guessed.

Pierce shrugged. "Of us seven brothers, I was the last to stay on the farm. Last I saw Bill, I was six and he was teaching me to ride. He lifted me in front of him in the saddle and I thought I was on top of the world. But Bill's heart was not in farming and he went away. The last letter we got from him said he was sheriff here."

McCarthy chuckled. "He still is. I'm his deputy and for the moment the only lawman in town if you don't want to consider Jeremiah and you don't, believe me. Bill went to Centennial yesterday. We had a problem there."

"How long will he be gone?" Pierce asked disappointed. Now that he had confirmation that his brother lived here, he was eager to meet him.

"A couple of days, who knows? These things are unpredictable." McCarthy rose and poured some coffee from a pot in his empty mug. He raised his mug in a mute invitation to Pierce, but the younger man shook his head. He'd had plenty of the bitter brew on the road. In winter, a hot drink was welcome, but now it was summer. No need for more hot drinks.

McCarthy returned to his desk. The young man in front of him was naïve and untried. Usually, he steered clear of such added complication. Life offered him plenty of trouble as it was. But he had no choice in this case. The young Monroe was his responsibility until Bill returned and he had to keep an eye on him. "You can bunk with me," he said pointing at an open door nearby.

"In jail?" Pierce asked looking in there.

"It is a jail room, but Bill and I use it to sleep once in a while when work keeps us longer into the night or when events in town might get rowdy and peace is threatened. Bill has a house in town, but frankly, I prefer to sleep here instead of the boarding house where I rent a room."

"In that case, I accept. Until Bill comes back. Thank you." Pierce looked outside through the window. The horse was waiting for him patiently in front. "Do you know where I could leave my buggy and where I could find feed for my horse?"

"You came from Kansas in a buggy?" the deputy

asked surprised.

"No. I came by train. I bought the buggy when I arrived here. Timmy, the clerk at the train depot, didn't know what to do with it and he sold it to me."

McCarthy didn't know if he should laugh or cry. By western standards, the boy, who was over twenty, should be able to stand on his own in the world, but he was greener than McCarthy had thought. A buggy? Only women and the doctor used buggies. Even the pastor used a more practical wagon.

"We have a small stable in the back. My horse is there. You can find oats for your horse there." He rose and went to look outside. To his relief the buggy didn't have all the pink fringes that women preferred or the kid would become the laughingstock in town. One look at the horse and McCarthy was surprised. He knew good horseflesh when he saw it and the horse harnessed at the buggy was an excellent riding horse. "How much did you pay for the horse?"

"Ten dollars for the horse and buggy together," Pierce said on his way out.

THE YOUNGER BROTHER

McCarthy blinked. All right, maybe the kid was no fool. Shaking his head, he chuckled and started reading the newspaper again.

Tom Wilkes, the owner of one of the popular saloons in town leaned over the railing and looked downstairs with satisfaction. It was going to be a good night. There were quite a lot of men at the bar, and not all were the usual drunkards in town. They were drinking whiskey, their eyes glued to the painting above the grand mirror behind the bar. Tom had paid a pretty penny for the painting called 'Danae'. The figure from Greek mythology it was supposed to represent, was quite well endowed, a woman with voluptuous charms, some only suggested, but not entirely revealed by the thin veil she was wearing. She was sitting on a velvet sofa, smiling beguilingly. Tom often wondered if the ancient Greeks had velvet sofas, but he decided that it didn't matter because the woman was quite fetching.

The two new girls he'd hired all the way from St.Louis were a plus, pushing the patrons to drink without being obvious and they mingled a lot, giving all of them equal attention. The piano player was playing a lively medley of songs. He was much better than the last one, who had a very limited repertoire.

The usual cards players and a few new faces were enjoying their game on the new tables Tom had ordered recently to replace the ones broken in the last brawl. He hoped these would last longer.

One of the card players, just arrived in town, was studying his partners with attention. It seemed that luck was on his side tonight. Across the table from him was a young man who looked picture-perfect the dupe he needed to pluck of all his money. And he had money, the card shark was sure. He'd seen him taking out of his pocket a bunch of paper money to pay for his drink. The other two players at the table didn't count, an older rancher who would fold before leaving too much of his money on the table and a younger cowboy who didn't have too much to his name, only the weekly pay probably.

The card shark pulled out of his pocket his

marked deck of cards and after expertly shuffling them, he dealt them. The game heated up soon and after an hour the pot was quite large.

The card shark offered the cards to his partner on the right, the cowboy, to cut. Clumsy, the cowboy dropped one card on the floor, but picked it up and placed it at the bottom of the deck. After the cards were dealt, the card player studied his hand and after placing the cards face-down on the table, he pushed all the money in front of him on the table, announcing his bet. As he anticipated, the rancher folded immediately, a man careful with his money. The cowboy looked at the pot, then at his hand and disappointed he folded too.

The young man pulled more money from his pocket and called. "Full house," he announced.

The card shark slowly raised his hand from the table. After years of playing he experienced the same rush of pleasure knowing he'd best his opponent in the game and he could leave with the pot. He placed the cards fanned face-up. "Four aces," he announced watching with attention to see the other one's face crumble when understanding sunk in that he had lost.

To his surprise, the younger man frowned and shook his head. "It's not possible. The ace of spades is at the bottom of the deck." He pointed at the cowboy. "He placed it there after he picked it up from the floor."

A vein started pulsing at the cards player's temple. "Are you accusing me of cheating?"

Unaware of the danger, the young man looked at the cards on the table. "Yes, there was no way…"

Instantly, the card player drew a gun and shot at the young man, who was watching his move and dropped under the table a fraction of a second before the bullet could hit him. Then another shot rang out and the gun flew from the card player's hand. He cried and grabbed his hand, although he had not been wounded.

Deputy Sheriff, Gabe McCarthy, placed his gun back in his holster and approached the table. All the talk and music stopped in the saloon and people turned to see what was going on.

"He accused me of cheating, Sheriff," the card player complained.

THE YOUNGER BROTHER

"And I'm sure you didn't," McCarthy said calmly, motioning for Pierce to step aside. Then he took his seat at the table. "Gentlemen," he said inviting the other two to take their seat.

"But you never play poker, Deputy," one of them said surprised.

Gabe pushed the old cards to the side and signaled to Tom to bring a new deck of cards. "I'll make an exception tonight. One game, all or nothing. Considering this is a debated pot, I will play for it."

Tom brought a new deck of cards and the people in the saloon all watched in surprise as the usually card-abstinent deputy shuffled them expertly. The card player had a bad feeling that his luck was at an end, but it was a large pot at stake and the gambler in him couldn't give it up. Besides, he was curious to find out if the deputy was a better player than him.

McCarthy gave the cards to the rancher to cut. Then he dealt the cards. The card player asked for three cards, and McCarthy picked one.

The card player was too versed not to keep a

straight face, but his heart fluttered when he saw a third king near his first two. Too bad the other two were not of the same to make a flush. Still he'd won some other times with worse cards.

The pot was on the table so there was no betting.

"Three kings," the card player announced triumphantly.

McCarthy took his time to look at his own hand and to place it on the table face-up. "Flush." The saloon erupted in cheering. No one had expected their deputy to best a card player who did this for a living.

But the deputy was focused on the card player. "This is my town. And we don't like foul play. I expect you to be on the first train out of here tomorrow."

The card player opened his mouth to protest. McCarthy looked at the cards still fanned with the four aces visible in the corner of the table. Then he turned the whole old deck upside down. There on top was the ace of spades.

The card player snapped his mouth shut and hastened to leave the saloon.

McCarthy turned to Pierce. "How much did you say you lost?"

"Two hundred eighty-five."

The deputy counted from the pot the exact sum of money and handed it back to Pierce. Then he rose to go.

"Wait, deputy," Tom Wilkes called him. "What about the rest of the money that you won?"

"Give it back to the people who lost it," McCarthy replied and left the saloon, disappearing into the night.

CHAPTER 3

"I'm sorry," Pierce mumbled in the darkness of the room.

"Kid, I'm not your Pa to tell you how to live your life," Gabe answered from his own narrow bed. "I just thought Bill won't be happy to find his little brother killed when he returns from Centennial."

It was possible that after twenty years his brother wouldn't care about what happened to Pierce. He might not even remember him. Then Pierce remembered the laughing man who had lifted him up in the saddle in front of him and who had encouraged him to dream and hope; that man would certainly care. At least, he'd be upset that Pierce was such a dunce to sit at the table with a card cheater. He sighed. "You're right. Bill will be mad with me. I wanted to live a little, like men in town do, drink a glass of whiskey, sit at the table with other men and play a hand of poker. And instead…"

"Instead, you were a nice prey for the card shark. It was a good lesson for you not to play cards in the future, and if you do, know very well who your partners are and what they are doing with the cards."

"How come you don't play, but you knew what the gambler was doing?" Pierce asked genuinely curious about this enigmatic man that was Bill's deputy.

"It takes one to know one," McCarthy answered, raising more questions instead of simply explaining. "Now it's time to sleep. I have to make rounds in town in two hours to ensure everything is quiet."

"Can I come with you?"

"No, you can't. You've had enough excitement for one night."

There was no way that Pierce could sleep after all he'd been through this day, starting with the robbers that had attacked the train.

"Gabe, were you a gambler, you know, a card shark?"

"You ask too many questions. It might get you in trouble here in the west, where people like their privacy and most have dark secrets in their past they would like to keep buried." There was a long moment of silence.

Only the crickets could be heard outside in the warm summer night. "I had to earn a living and it seemed card player was better than being a gun for hire. Besides, it gave me the right cover to find out what I wanted to know and to follow the person I was searching for."

"You've been a lawman," Pierce guessed.

"I've been a Texas Ranger and then a marshal at some point in my life, but not always. The last man I was looking for, it was for a personal reason."

"What reason?"

"He killed an old friend of mine, who was prospecting for gold in Colorado," McCarthy replied lost in thought.

Pierce guessed this happened quite recently. "Was Bill with you when you caught him?" he wanted to know.

"No, his previous deputy was. The woman he loved was the sister of the outlaw holed up in Medicine Bow Mountains, near Centennial."

"Did you… did you kill him?" Pierce asked breathless.

"No. A man who thought the outlaw betrayed their secret business deal shot him dead. But I was ready to do it myself and I told him so and why. You have to be careful Pierce, when a man becomes intent on killing there is little difference, if any, between killing for a righteous reason and doing it for personal gain. Promise me, to do it only to defend yourself."

That was an unusual demand. Pierce had no intention of killing anyone ever. Then he thought of the gambler who'd wanted to kill him just for revealing that he'd cheated. Sometimes he might not have a choice. "I promise," he agreed.

"Good, because tomorrow we're going to a range out of town and I'll teach you to shoot."

Pierce was ambiguous about going shooting. He didn't want to have to shoot anyone, but he had to admit that sometimes life gave you no choice. In such cases, it was better to know what you were doing. "We're going shooting, really?" he asked. A soft snore was his answer. The deputy had fallen asleep.

The next morning, the deputy was called to the Wyoming Territorial Prison to talk to the two marshals who'd caught the train robbers. It looked like there had been four, not three robbers, and one had escaped.

The shooting was postponed for the afternoon. Left alone, Pierce decided to visit the town. The recently installed electricity left him confused. It was progress and it had been adopted by some of the larger cities. Laramie was the first small town west of Mississippi to have an electric plant built in 1886. It was only the beginning. Electric light was provided at a very dear price to some of the main streets in town and to the few businesses and private residences that could afford it. Pierce was not sure if the wires hanging between the buildings and at the top of tall posts were an improvement to the convenient gas lamps. Of course, it was less smelly and less fumigating, but was it an improvement? Many people were skeptical, not just Pierce.

Trabing Commercial Co. store impressed him much more. His Pa took him once to the mercantile in

THE YOUNGER BROTHER

Dodge City and he had been surprised by the large variety of merchandise, but this store surpassed by far any mercantile he'd seen. The sheer size of it and the way the merchandise was displayed on shelves and islands to tempt the buyers with much more items than what they intended to buy originally. It was grand.

It was a warm pleasant summer day and Pierce enjoyed walking on the boardwalk to the train depot.

"Hey Timmy, no more robbers on today's train or other unpleasant events?" he asked his friend from the day before.

"No, not today." Timmy smiled at him and then hastened back inside where he was called by the stationmaster.

Hmm. Everyone was busy and Pierce felt the odd duck out, not having any business to do. As soon as Bill returned from that Centennial, whatever town that was, Pierce would look for a job or something useful to do and earn his living. Maybe Bill had some suggestions about that.

Close to the train depot, there was an old, dusty

building. 'Mercantile' was written on a sign, which was hanging lopsided above the door. Curious, Pierce entered. It was dark and grungy inside, with merchandise placed one on top of another on the shelves and on what Pierce assumed was the counter, now invisible under the burden of bolts of fabric, boxes with nails and other items more in demand. On top of it all, there was a pair of work boots that an old cowboy had just tried on and was haggling over the price with a grumpy older man, presumably the owner of the shop.

Pierce was ignored as would have been any other shopper. He wondered if the mercantile made any profit at all in such conditions and with the Trabing store a mighty competitor. The only way the old man could survive in business was if he sold his stuff really cheap and considering the ongoing conversation with the cowboy that was not the case.

Oh well, each to his own business, Pierce thought, leaving the mercantile quickly. At the corner of the building, he turned and plowed into a boy who came running from the opposite direction. The collision was unexpected and hard and the boy grabbed Pierce's sleeve to steady himself, unbalancing him. They would have fallen on the boardwalk if not for the building. The boy leaned against the wall, with Pierce against him.

"Get off me, you oaf," the boy said in an unmistakably feminine voice full of outrage.

Maybe he was young and his voice had not changed yet, Pierce thought. The curves flattened against his chest felt distinctly female though.

He saw the exact moment when her eyes widened, aware that Pierce had discovered she was not a boy. With a cry, she pushed him away and vanished behind the building.

Pierce thought to chase after her, but for what purpose? She was already scared out of her wits. Maybe it was his fault for not paying attention where he was walking so fast. He traced his steps back to the front of the mercantile and sat on a wooden bench placed right there on the boardwalk.

He intended to take only a few moments before returning to the Sheriff's Office. A slight noise to his right, at the corner of the building, alerted him that he was not alone. Out of the corner of his eye he saw the now familiar cap pulled low on the boy's head and the rather worn clothes.

Not knowing what to do he started talking. "A very wise man told me yesterday that people here out west like their privacy respected and not many questions asked. Rest assured that your secret is safe with me. I don't know you and I'm not about to trumpet it all over town."

"Who was the wise man?" The question was a faint whisper.

"Gabe McCarthy, the sheriff's deputy."

The girl dressed in boy's clothes came forward and sat down on the boardwalk near the bench, circling her knees with her thin arms. Her clothes were ragged.

"I believe you. I have no choice. I never did."

"I'm a good listener if you need to talk. My own family died of typhus and I had to sell the farm. I traveled from Kansas here to meet my brother. I am lucky he still lives here, but he was away from town. I'm

Pierce Monroe," he said, making no move to turn to her or to look at her.

"Your brother is Sheriff Monroe?" she asked surprised.

"Yep. I haven't seen him in twenty years."

She nodded. "He's a good man. He saved me one evening when I was cornered by some drunkards at the saloon. Another one in his place wouldn't have bothered."

Pierce wondered what she was doing at the saloon in the evening even dressed as a boy. Not his business, he remembered himself. "Ma raised us boys to respect women," he said instead.

"He had no idea then that I was a woman. He saw the cowboys harassing the boy who cleaned at the saloon and made mincemeat of them. 'No man worth his salt will bully a weaker and smaller person just because he can,' he told them. He was the first man who defended me in all my life." She smiled a little embarrassed. "I guess I fell in love with him then."

"With Bill?" Pierce squeaked.

"Yeah, he's worth loving. But he is in love with that fancy lady from Baltimore who was on the last stagecoach to Centennial with him. Now, her parents came and she returned east without a glance back. Life is like that," she concluded and dusting herself off rose to go.

CHAPTER 4

"Wait," Pierce called after her. "If you have a few moments more, tell me about Bill. I didn't want to ask the deputy about his sheriff. I'm new in town and I have no friend to talk to." Now he sounded pathetic, but the young woman, dressed like a ragamuffin was no better.

She was undecided, but she returned next to him. "I'm more partial to the sheriff than his deputy. I just told you why. From my point of view, he can do no wrong. He is a good man, strong and fast to punish those who break the law." She smiled widely at some thought that crossed her mind.

"Hey, don't do that," Pierce admonished her looking around to see if anyone was watching them. "When you smile like that and your entire face lights up, you are so pretty that no man would believe you're a poor boy."

"Oh," she said digesting what he said. "I never thought of that because no one ever told me that I'm pretty."

"Why not? What about your family?" Pierce asked curious, forgetting his promise not to ask personal questions or to pry in another's private life.

It seemed that she was also in need of a friend to unburden her sadness, and she started to talk. "I was born in Chicago and I was an orphan since I was a little girl. My uncle took me in and I worked as a servant doing whatever was asked of me, from cleaning rooms to helping in the kitchen."

Pierce made a sound of compassion, so she raised her hand. "No, it was not all bad, not at all. I had a small room in the attic that was warm and the housekeeper and the cook were two kind women who took me under their wing. They were my family. When I was eighteen, my uncle called me in his office and told me that from the next day I was to go to a lecherous old man, business associate of his."

"He wanted you to marry an old man?" Pierce was outraged.

"No, not to marry. I was only a servant without importance after all. I was supposed to serve the other man who paid him a good sum of money for my services. And cleaning was not what he had in mind."

Pierce looked at her horrified. "What did you do?"

"What could I do? I ran away in the middle of the night. I had no money because being a relative I was not paid like a servant. The housekeeper and the cook gave me some money and also they had this idea that I'd be safer dressed as a boy."

"Where did you go?"

"As far away from Chicago as I could. I wanted to go to San Francisco. I thought there were many rich residences there in need of a hardworking servant," she explained.

"So, how did you end up in Laramie, Wyoming?"

"Simple. I ran out of money. I stopped here planning to earn some money and then continue my journey."

"By cleaning the saloon? Couldn't you find another place to work at?" As soon as he voiced the question, Pierce regretted it. He sounded critical and he didn't mean to be judgmental.

"I did, even at the Kuster Hotel. But this meant to rent a room at the boarding house. It was more expensive than what I could afford and the lady was quite nosy and she wouldn't accept me as a boy. At the saloon, the girls are generous and there is a small room under the stairs, used for storage. It is only slightly bigger than a closet, but the girls brought a cot inside. It has a sturdy lock and it is my paradise where I can relax and sleep without fear."

Pierce nodded. "I see. How long before you save enough for your train ticket?" He knew he'd regret to see his new friend go, but that was life. People went where they thought their future was going to be better.

"I have the money, but…" she hesitated, then she raised her big brown eyes at him. "I discovered that I have more ambition to succeed and I'm apprenticing to be a milliner." Seeing Pierce's doubtful look, she grabbed his hand and pulled him off the bench and into the street. "Here, I'll show you."

Pierce yanked his hand back like burned. "Hey,

men don't go hand in hand."

She smiled sheepishly. "Sorry, I forgot. I'm Amy. Amy Poole."

They rounded the corner of 1st and Grand and then Amy stopped not far from there. He saw a dressmaker's shop, and right near it, there was a milliner's store. The window presented a large hat with a lot of colorful silk flowers that could have covered an entire meadow and blue ribbons and feathers. Amy looked at it reverently, in awe and said with a sigh, "Isn't this a marvelous confection?"

Pierce scratched his head and placed his hat back. "I don't know, Amy. I don't think it's practical for the ranchers' wives or even simple women in town. Even the saloon girls won't need this because they live and stay mostly inside."

"I know that. Miss Priscilla said that we need an eye-catching hat for the window to attract people's eyes. Do you think a simple straw hat with a blue ribbon would bring in customers? No, it would not. But this one does. Miss Priscilla had an even more colorful one before, but a famous singer traveling through town bought it. We don't expect this to be bought anytime soon. But it will…"

Whatever Amy wanted to say was interrupted by the exit from the store of a young elegant woman, dressed in a fetching dress of yellow and burgundy stripes with yellow silk top. She pulled the door shut with more force than necessary and her blue eyes sparkled with unrepressed anger. She stopped outside and measured Pierce and Amy up and down with contempt. She made a huffing sound of irritation and shaking her blond curls she climbed in an ornate buggy with a pink fringe and ribbons on top. She grabbed the whip and expertly shook the ribbons and with the other hand struck the horse hard.

Amy winced when the horse jumped forward at the strike and then pulled the buggy away at a fast pace.

"Wow!" Pierce said his eyes glued to the departing figure driving the buggy. "That is the most beautiful woman I've ever seen in my life. She's like an angel," he observed remembering the sweetly rounded face framed by golden curls, the small bow-arched pink lips and slightly upturned delicate nose and the flashing blue eyes with long eyelashes a shade darker than her hair. She was perfection.

"Beautiful is as beautiful does," Amy commented with rancor. "And this is a bad one. She treats Miss Priscilla like she is dirt under her soles. She changes her mind without any consideration for the hours of work to create the hats. You'd think she's the queen of... something. And she's not. Shopkeepers have respect for fussy customers who are rich and pay for what they want. Miss Vanessa is not. Her Pa is a manager on one of the ranches nearby and he doesn't have money for her expensive tastes. So she bargains for every piece of ribbon and tries to get it cheaper."

Pierce frowned. "You seem very set against her. Did she do anything to you?"

"She slapped me once." Amy shrugged. "I was a poor boy without importance in the grand scheme of her life."

Yes, that was bad and Pierce felt sorry for his

new friend. Perhaps the goddess had been upset or there must have been an explanation surely and this was not her common behavior. Long after, her face persisted in Pierce's mind and he couldn't forget her.

Later in the afternoon, Deputy McCarthy and Pierce rode to a place outside of town, across from the train tracks to practice target shooting. McCarthy arranged a variety of bottles and tin cans at a distance and explained to Pierce how to handle the Colt he borrowed from the Sheriff's Office.

Both of them were rather distracted and their attention was not into target practice. McCarthy was worried about the wounded robber that escaped from the two marshals and was running loose in the area. And Pierce was thinking of the gorgeous woman that captivated his imagination thoroughly like no other before. Not that he had the opportunity to meet such sophisticated ladies in the Kansas countryside where he'd lived until now.

After wasting the first round of bullets shooting

far from the targets, he followed McCarthy's instructions and paying better attention to each makeshift target, he hit them all except two.

McCarthy's eyes widened and he chuckled. "How did you do so well? I was just thinking you're hopeless."

"Ma said my eyes were better than any other man's. Perhaps that helped."

"I think it did. What you have to do now is practice your speed to draw. You don't want to be surprised be a fast drawing crook who wants to eliminate you from whatever game he's playing, not only of cards. In a confrontation, pay attention not what the opponent is saying, but at a higher pitch in his voice or a narrowing of his eyes. Such signs will tell you he's about to draw. You have to do it a fraction of a second faster if you want to be the one surviving the confrontation."

Pierce looked at the blue sky and at a bird flying high and asked Gabe an unexpected question. "Deputy, have you ever been in love?"

That was the last thing McCarthy wanted to talk about. He made a grimace and tried to look severe.

"Didn't you learn anything about westerners, kid?"

"Yeah, I did. They don't like people prying. I haven't met Bill yet, but somehow I don't imagine me having such talk with him. At least not now. Maybe later, when I'll get to know him better and be more at ease with him."

"But you imagine talking to me," McCarthy concluded, not knowing if he should be glad that the younger man trusted him or to be annoyed that he'd been chosen as a source of confessions of the heart.

"Well, yeah. I don't know anyone in town except you and Amy."

"Who's Amy?"

Pierce realized his faux pas and tried to diffuse McCarthy's interest. "No one important."

"Kid…."

"And please don't call me 'kid'. I'm twenty-six."

McCarthy looked at him in disbelief. The kid was only a few years younger than him. He looked so much younger and innocent compared to Gabe who felt old and used, considering all the life experience he had. "Very well," he conceded. "Anyhow it was not meant in a derogatory way. Let's see. When I was eighteen and already two years on my own and with several gunfights under my belt, I fell in love with a woman who worked in a saloon. I was so much in love that my inattention to whatever else happened around me almost got me killed. It cured me of lovesick sighs, especially as the lady had rejected me over and over. I left town and a year later I heard by chance that she died of consumption. End of story."

"How sad!" Pierce remarked.

"Nah. It's one of the hard lessons life teaches you. Don't fall in love. It's not worth it. It makes you vulnerable and it might get you killed."

CHAPTER 5

Pierce and the deputy were having breakfast in a companionable silence, each one lost in thought. It had been a peaceful night, no drunken brawls or robbed stores. McCarthy's rounds had been uneventful. Of course he knew that such peace was rare and could change at any given moment.

The door opened and a tall, somber looking man entered. He wore a long duster despite the sunny warm weather outside.

"I rode all night and I'm beaten," he growled and went to the stove in the corner to pour himself coffee in an empty tin cup. "The new mine manager seems to be a tad better than the previous one. Bad news, the outlaws are still there in the Medicine Bow Mountains and I couldn't find their new hole. I'll have to go again." He turned to Gabe. "Has the Baltimore Sun paper arrived?"

"It sure did, Bill. It's right here in your drawer. And also your younger brother from Kansas arrived," McCarthy said polishing his plate and drinking the last drop of his coffee. He figured the brothers needed time alone for a proper reunion.

Pierce, who was studying intently the newcomer, rose from his chair smiling and with his arms open. "Bill…"

His brother's somber look didn't change and it didn't encourage a warm hug. "Which one are you?" he asked only mildly curious, definitely too tired to bother showing more interest.

Pierce closed his eyes for a second. The lively image of the smiling young man who lifted him in the saddle in front of him, blurred and fizzled. The young man he remembered was no more. He'd been naïve to think and hope otherwise. His mistake. "I'm Pierce, the youngest," he said sadly, his arms falling back at his side. There would be no warm welcome and embrace.

"Hmm, and what do you want, Pierce? Money, a job, what? Because I'll tell you right now there is no easy way in life and nothing is for free," the sheriff said continuing to sip his coffee.

"Now, Bill, the kid didn't say…" McCarthy tried

to intervene. He realized that the sheriff was double upset, once for the wasted ride to Centennial, and second for the unrequited love for the Baltimore woman. But this didn't justify the harsh treatment of his younger brother.

"Stop, stop both of you," Pierce shouted. "I'm not a kid, I told you I'm twenty-six." He turned to Bill. "I didn't come asking for any favors. You talk about the easy way out? You all, who left all responsibility behind and went to find your way in life? I was the only one who worked hard to make a living and keep the farm afloat. I was there when both Ma and Pa got sick and died of typhus. I fought the banker who came to claim that Pa had an unpaid debt and wanted to foreclose. I found papers and proof that any debt was long paid off and the farm was ours free and clear. And yes, after all this, I got tired of fighting for it and I sold it to our neighbor. There was no one there to help me for years. I didn't come here expecting help." He made a disgusted waving gesture with his hand and went outside pulling the door shut after him.

THE YOUNGER BROTHER

Gabe McCarthy breathed deeply and told himself it was not his problem and he shouldn't interfere. But the kid's disappointed face swam in front of his eyes and he couldn't refrain from talking. "What's gotten into you, Bill? It's not like you to be mean or to hurt the kid's feelings. I know you're frustrated. If it's that fancy Baltimore woman you want, why don't you take the train east and go ask her to marry you. Considering the pieces she writes in the paper about the brave Wyoming sheriff, I think she's ready to say yes."

"Out of the question," the sheriff replied morosely. "I went once to propose and I was showed the… stairs, not even the door because I was not received inside by her father. He cured me by any desire to dream of a woman so above me."

"Maybe she didn't know."

"She left the next day with her parents without a polite Good-bye at least."

McCarthy ruffled his short blond hair in exasperation. "This is no reason to treat Pierce like you did. He is a good kid. He was left alone in the world and hoped to reconnect with his older brother. That's all he wants."

The sheriff looked in his empty cup and set it on the desk. "Look, I'm not heartless, but this young man who claims to be my brother…"

The deputy frowned. "Do you doubt he is?"

"No, he is my younger brother. But he has gullible written all over him."

McCarthy remembered how the young man lost his money and almost lost his life at the poker table. "In this you might be right," he conceded.

"Life is hard," the sheriff continued. "Being nice and soft with him I'll make him no favors. On the contrary. It will give him a false sense of security that simply doesn't exist. He needs to toughen up."

McCarthy shook his head, but didn't reply. He disagreed with this man, one of the few that he had ever counted among his friends. He thought that young Pierce would benefit from the affection and advice from an older friend or from his brother.

"Life's hardship makes us grow up and mature.

THE YOUNGER BROTHER

Both you and I have been alone from a younger age and learned to fight our own battles." Bill Monroe took off his duster and then he wiped his face with a napkin on the desk. He was bone-tired and he didn't need this extra issue to worry about. "I'll tell you what I'll do. I'll give him a chance to prove he's a man."

The door opened again and Pierce came in. "My horse is ready. I have to take my trunk," he said explaining to Gabe.

The sheriff leaned back in the chair and measured Pierce. "I have a job for you if you want to prove…"

"I don't have to prove anything to you," Pierce said, with the natural defiance of the youth.

"Don't be so hasty. Wait till you hear. I have a ranch." Bill Monroe remembered again the weird turn of events that led to his acquiring the ranch and a ghost of a smile crossed his face.

In spite of himself, Pierce was intrigued. "A ranch? Why would you buy a ranch? You could have our family farm if you were interested in working the land. But you never were."

"I didn't exactly buy it. A young man inherited it and he didn't want it. He wanted to leave town but I couldn't let him because in a drunken moment he shot and broke the big mirror at Tom Wilkes' saloon."

Gabe McCarthy guffawed. "I would have liked to see that."

Pierce looked from one to the other confused. "What does the broken mirror at the saloon got to do with the ranch?"

"The story has more details than this, but bottom line is that the young man offered to give the deed to the ranch to me in exchange for my paying for the mirror and letting him leave town with the earliest train."

"He could have sold it," Gabe reflected practically.

"Not that evening, no. And he had good reasons for wanting to be on the next day's train."

"What did you do with the ranch?" Pierce asked.

"At first nothing. Then, because there were some cattle left there from the previous owner, I hired a man to take care of it."

Pierce shrugged. "All right, I guess. If you don't like to take care of it, it's better than doing nothing and let it fall into ruin."

The sheriff pretended to study his empty cup of coffee. "This is where you come in. I was thinking you could go there to supervise how the work goes."

It was Gabe who intervened. "No, Bill. Warner is a devil. You know that. His men are gunslingers, not cowboys. This is no job for the kid."

The sheriff cut his word. "So? I meant to go there and make order and fire Warner. Then what? Find another greedy crook to manage the ranch?"

"I'll do it," Pierce said without any hesitation.

"Listen, kid, you don't know what vipers' nest is there," Gabe tried to temper him down. In his opinion getting rid of the crook manager was more of a job for the sheriff with a handful of seasoned men able to fight. The kid would get in trouble and it could turn ugly for him.

Pierce raised his hand. "Since I'm not going there as your brother, but, as you said, as a supervisor I want a paper saying that you give me full authority to take what measures I consider necessary to improve the activity on the ranch. And the second condition is, if I succeed getting rid of the bad men nestled there and if I make the ranch prosperous, or at least efficient, I want half of the ranch, which doesn't interest you anyhow."

Both Gabe and the sheriff looked at him surprised.

"You don't ask much, do you?" Bill said.

Pierce shrugged. "As Gabe said this is not easy task. At least he was honest and warned me what to expect, unlike you, who had no hesitation to send me into danger without telling me about it."

"It was a test for you and your ability to survive."

"Yes, well, Whatever your reasons were, these are my conditions. Take it or leave it. An able bodied man can find work anytime, anywhere. Nothing holds me here."

"You drive a hard bargain," the sheriff said pretending to consider it. "If you can chase away that gang of thieves from my land, I'll deed the ranch over to you. After all, I don't need it, and easy come, easy go, as they say."

Pierce looked at him intently. "You don't think I'll succeed. You think I'll fail." Yes, that's exactly what his big brother thought. Pierce looked at the deputy and read compassion and regret, but also the same kind of doubt he saw on Bill's face. "I'm going to take my trunk and you write that authorization. Do we have a deal about the ranch? Let's shake on it. Gabe is witness." He extended his hand. For a moment he thought his brother would either ignore his hand or would try a contest of who could squeeze harder. He was prepared for both.

But Bill shook his hand simply and when Pierce looked in his brother's eyes he thought he saw a flicker of respect. Then it was gone. It had been only in his imagination, he was sure.

He went next door and retrieved his trunk and carried it outside to the buggy and tied it to the back where there was a flat support for it. Then he entered again the Sheriff's Office. Without a word Bill handed him the written authorization. Pierce looked over it and found it acceptable. He nodded and turned to go.

"Hey kid, you might need this where you're going." Gabe threw him the holster with the Colt he used the day before.

Yes, he might need it. No point being stubborn. Pierce buckled it to his waist, smiled at Gabe and left the office without looking back at his brother.

CHAPTER 6

His trunk was strapped at the back of the buggy and the horse waited patiently the signal to move along. Pierce patted his neck. "It's only you and I. Alone as usual."

The door to the Sheriff's Office opened and Gabe came out. "Pierce. Take care." He seemed uneasy about what to say to this honest young man, who was going straight into a dangerous situation. He'd gotten to know and like him in the short time since they'd met. "He's a good man," Gabe finally said inclining his head toward the Sheriff's Office. "Tough, but fair - a good man."

Pierce looked at him. "Good man. Go figure. He reminds me of my father. All our neighbors and the people who knew him agreed that he was a good man. He never raised his hand to strike Ma or me. But he didn't show us an ounce of affection and he used to put us down every day, making us believe that he almost hated us."

"You don't have to judge Bill so harshly. His life

has not been easy lately." Gabe patted Pierce awkwardly on the arm. He was not a man used to affection either. Nobody showed it to him, and he had no idea how to be affectionate to others. Maybe the sheriff was right. The west was not a place for affection. "Listen, if you are in trouble, don't hesitate, send someone to us and we'll come to your help immediately."

"Thank you, Gabe. I appreciate your care, but you know I can't do it. This was not the deal. I have to succeed there alone, no matter how big the danger is." He smiled his lopsided sad smile, now so familiar to Gabe, fit his floppy hat on his head and vaulted up in the buggy. Then he turned to Gabe. "If I could impose one more time on your kindness, I want to ask you to keep an eye on a poor boy cleaning at Tom Wilkes' saloon. I'm afraid for her... hmm... him. He's my friend and what with me away at the ranch I don't know who will take care of Amy."

"I'll watch out for him/her whatever his story is. I promise." Gabe intended not only to keep his promise, but to find out more about Pierce's friend. Because if what he guessed was right and this young girl was working at the saloon posing as a boy, she faced unsavory characters every day and her safety was at risk there.

A genuine smile bloomed on Pierce's face this time. "Thank you for everything." And with this he took the reins in his hands and drove away. Knowing that Amy had Gabe watching over her, made him feel at peace about her at least.

Trying to chase away the anxiety he felt, he paid more attention to his surroundings. The town was growing. The railroad was an artery that pulsed new life in this western town. New people and businesses arrived in Laramie every day.

Pierce looked for the road that would take him northwest of town. At a corner of the street he saw an older woman with a hat full of fake cherries trembling at every movement of her head. She looked woebegone and ready to cry, wringing her hands, like not knowing what to do.

After he drove past her, Pierce thought she, or

better said - her hat, looked vaguely familiar. He stopped the buggy near the boardwalk and jumped down. He ran back to her. She was still there at the corner of the street.

"Mrs. Heller," he called her. She looked at him confused. "It's me, Pierce Monroe. From the train," he added hoping to refresh her memory.

"Oh, Pierce. Of course I remember you. How are you?"

"I could be better, but I don't complain. What about you? You seem upset."

Mrs. Heller's eyes filled with tears. "I found out that my son has died, a few months ago, somewhere at a mine where he was working. Foolish old woman that I am, I thought it would be a nice surprise to come here. Now, I don't have money to go to see where he is buried or to return back East and the landlady at the boardinghouse needs my room. She barely makes a living as it is." She sniffed and wiped her eyes in a white handkerchief. "Don't worry about me. I'll manage. I'm in good health for my age and I'm a fairly good cook. I tried a few places, but they didn't need my services.

That's why I was discouraged."

It was heartbreaking to see an older woman crying. Pierce didn't need to think twice about it. "Come with me. I'm going to a place where the people might not be friendly, so it could be dangerous, but I have the authority to offer you a place to live for the moment." He guided her to his buggy while telling her about the whole deal he'd made with his brother. At the end of the story, he had to admit it was not such a great offer he had for the poor Mrs. Heller. "I understand if you choose to stay in the relative safety of the town," he concluded.

Mrs. Heller looked better, quite animated in fact. "Are you kidding? Of course I'm coming with you. You need someone with you there, to take care of you."

Pierce smiled. Mrs. Heller was a nurturer, just like his Ma. She needed to take care of people in order to be happy. "Let's go to take your trunk from the boardinghouse, Mrs. Heller."

"Call me Edith dear."

Years of instructions about polite behavior drone on by his mother, made Pierce hesitate to such familiar address.

"Or how about Aunt Edith?" she amended.

"Aunt Edith, hmm?" he tested the sound on his tongue. "I like it. I never had an aunt before."

"Then it's high time you had one," she said arranging her skirts on the buggy's bench.

After collecting Mrs. Heller's trunk from the boardinghouse and strapping it on top of Pierce's smaller one, they were on their way to the ranch. The sky was bright blue and the sun was shining and warming the land. It was a glorious Wyoming summer day.

"Beautiful country," Mrs. Heller observed, enjoying the shade that the top of the buggy provided. "Not many trees here, very different from back East, but much less crowded and the wide open space is a welcoming change."

They had passed two other large ranches, the buildings just dots in the distance, when Pierce veered left off the country road marked by wagon wheel tracks and drove toward west past some boulders. There was no sign announcing the Monroe ranch. Pierce knew Bill didn't bother to mark his property or even to inspect it from time to time. No wonder the so-called manager was doing whatever he pleased.

"The house should be somewhere on our left. Perhaps we shall see it after we cross beyond those rocks."

The house was indeed there in the distance and so were three riders galloping fast toward them in a dusty cloud.

"The welcoming committee, I assume," Aunt Edith said sighing, but keeping her calm. She stuck her hand in her reticule.

"No, don't," Pierce placed his own hand on top of hers stopping her to get her gun out. "We have no chance against the three of them in a shoot-out. On their horses, they are more mobile than us sitting here on the buggy bench like sitting ducks."

"Look, they are shooting at us," Aunt Edith protested. "Let me clip one of them at least. I used to be a good shooter at county fairs back in Pennsylvania. I could always hit the moving turkey."

Pierce burst into spontaneous laughter just as the three riders stopped at a distance in front of them.

"Turn back. This is private property," the one in the middle told them. He had a hard time restraining his horse that was stomping and shaking his head like rearing to run further.

Pierce nodded. "Yes. It is the Monroe private property. This is Bar M, the Monroe Ranch. I'm Pierce Monroe and this here is Aunt Edith."

This made the man lose some of his self-assurance. He frowned. "Boss said no one is to come here without his permission."

"Boss is not the owner of this ranch," Pierce remarked.

This didn't deter another man, the one on the right, to raise his rifle and threaten them. "He also said we could shoot on site anyone who dares to ride onto the property. I don't care who you are. Boss pays me, I do his bidding."

"You could shoot us, of course," Aunt Edith said looking at him unruffled. "And you'll find the sheriff and a posse right on your tails."

The reminder that the rightful owner of the ranch was also the sheriff sobered them up some. "We'll go ask the Boss," the one in the middle, who seemed to be their leader, concluded. At his signal, they turned the horses around and rode hard toward the ranch house.

"Drive on," Aunt Edith said waving away from her face the dust left in the wake of the departing riders.

Aunt Edith proved to be an unexpected asset in his fight to regain control over Bill's ranch, Pierce thought, clicking his tongue for the horse to start moving on.

News of their arrival had spread fast and when Pierce stopped the buggy in front of the house, there was a short, stout middle aged man on the porch looking thunderous. He didn't say anything, just measured them with his beady eyes like a cougar ready to pounce.

Two could play this game, Pierce thought. He smiled widely and jumped down. He circled the buggy and helped Aunt Edith to climb down from it. He watched as she marched right on the porch.

"Out of my way," she said regally and pushing the man aside entered the house.

"What is the meaning of this?" the man asked Pierce, red-faced with anger and pushed past his limit.

"I think it's obvious. This is the Monroe Ranch and we're here to stay," Pierce said and hefting Aunt Edith trunk on his shoulder made his way up the stairs on the porch.

"I'm Pierce Monroe and I'll take care of this ranch for my brother, the sheriff." He extracted Bill's written authorization from his pocket and handed it to the man.

With undisguised fury the man snatched the paper and read it. "But I'm the manager," he said.

"Not anymore, you're not," Pierce replied calmly. The manager tore the paper in two and threw it on the ground. Pierce shook his head. "The fact is that from now on I'm in charge and by now the whole town knows it. You have ten days to leave the ranch with all your hired men."

"No way."

THE YOUNGER BROTHER

"A week then," Pierce told him over his shoulder making his way in, eager to drop Aunt Edith's trunk on the floor. He was young and strong, but the trunk was so heavy like it was packed with stones.

CHAPTER 7

No soon had he set the trunk down on the floor, that a younger woman came out of the kitchen wailing. "Ay de mi. The woman is crazy. She threw me out of the kitchen." She pushed past Pierce and struck the trunk with her foot. This elicited a louder wail while she was hopping around.

"Stop your caterwauling, woman," the manager told her from the porch, where he was puffing a cigar to calm his anger. He looked inside through the door. "Go to the bunkhouse and cook there."

Pierce hid his smile and picked up the trunk again. He was looking for a couple of empty rooms, one for Aunt Edith and one for himself. He opened the first door on the right. The spacious room was obviously designed to be a master bedroom. The present occupant was a man judging by the array of masculine items spread around the room. The furniture was finely crafted, of very good quality. He doubted it belonged to the rough manager. More likely the house was left ready furnished by the previous owner. A strong tobacco smell permeated every corner and Pierce thought the room would need a thorough cleaning and intense airing to get the smell out of it. Pierce was not a smoker and he didn't think either his brother, or his deputy were avid cigar smokers.

The next room took him by surprise with its cabbage roses wallpaper and the white delicate furniture. Did the manager have a wife or a mistress that he housed here at the Monroe Ranch? Pierce wondered. He was not sure if this would make his task easier or more difficult. In contrast to the first room, this one reeked of an exotic perfume that assailed Pierce's nostrils and made him sneeze violently, and he almost dropped the trunk.

At the end of the hallway he found what he was looking for. A good-size room, rather clean and sparsely furnished. It showed no signs of being occupied. This was perfect for Aunt Edith and Pierce set the trunk down.

Next room, across the hallway from the one with pink roses was a smaller one, which had been at one time either a nursery or a craft room. Useful, but too small for Pierce. Slowly he closed the door and looked inside the last room on the left, which had the door opened. This one was also a good size, and had adequate furniture. The bed was unmade and showed signs that someone slept here. No other personal objects showed that a person lived here permanently.

Pierce pulled a drawer of the chest open. There was bed linen there, not someone's underwear. He nodded satisfied and pulled the sheets from the bed. This would be his room. He left and stepped outside to bring his own trunk in.

To his surprise there was another buggy stopped near his own. One that was familiar, with fringes and pink ribbons on top.

And the beautiful proud woman who haunted his dreams was cursing and yelling. "Who was the idiot who left this buggy in front of the house? Papa, tell him to move from here. I need to unload my parcels."

Wasn't she something to behold? Pierce thought with admiration. She had quite a temper. He nodded at her. "I'll move the buggy just after I finish carrying in my trunk," he answered good-naturedly.

THE YOUNGER BROTHER

It looked like she was not used her wishes to be ignored. "You oaf, move it right now," she ordered and she snatched his hat and slapped him with it over the face. Then she threw it on the ground.

Slowly, he picked it up, dusted it off and set it back on his head. "As I said, I have to carry my trunk inside."

With the corner of his eye he sensed her move her hand. She raised it to strike him again. Pierce caught her wrist, forced it down and squeezed it a little, without exercising much force. Then he let it drop and turned away. The cloying perfume wafted his way and he twitched his nose to stop the incoming sneeze.

He hefted his trunk on his shoulder and stepped up on the porch. The ranch manager, Warner, continued to smoke his cigar and only raised an eyebrow at him, without comment.

Down in the yard, after a moment of stunned silence, the woman started cursing him again.

All things considered, it was not a bad day, Pierce

concluded later that night, thinking back at how the day had unfolded. Frankly, he'd expected a worse confrontation and he thought it'd continue at the dinner table. Instead, dinner was a peaceful affair, with Aunt Edith and Pierce eating at the large table in the kitchen, while the manager, his tempestuous daughter and two of his hired men dined in the front room.

Aunt Edith made very clear that while she cooked from the supplies found in the house, they were welcome to her food, but she was not their servant. In other words, they'll have to help themselves.

Pierce rubbed his eyes. It was late in the evening and he was reading an old favorite book left to him by his mother. The kerosene lamp flickered and the fumes irritated his eyes. He left his room and went into the parlor in search for another lamp, with more fuel and less prone to fumigating.

There was some light from the moon outside coming through the open window. He found the lamp on the table and was ready to return to his own room when he heard voices outside. Silently he went closer to the window.

"Papa, he is a nuisance, you must admit. Look how he left his buggy in front of the house like he owns the place. You have to get rid of him." A woman's whisper came to his hearing through the window with the night's breeze.

"It's not that simple. His brother is the sheriff." The manager's voice grunted.

"The sheriff doesn't care about this ranch that he won in a dubious deal, people say. And if he sent this country bumpkin here it means he doesn't care about him either." She tried to make her point. Her despise of him was so obvious that Pierce winced. It would take a lot to convince her of the contrary.

"Shh, not so loud. I have a plan. I'll make his life so miserable that he'll be happy to hightail out of here. I succeeded to dupe Crawford and he was a mean son of a gun. Unfortunately for him, he was obsessed with his ambition to own all the land north of Laramie. The more he bought, the more he wanted. Until he was killed."

"I know. By John Gorman. They say Gorman

never missed a target, he's that good with a gun." There was a wistful admiration in her voice.

"Yes, well. Gorman is a man I wouldn't want to be my enemy. As for this halfwit that the sheriff sent here, it is only a matter of time until he'll cry foul and run away. Nothing and no one will stay in the way of my plans. There is too much at stake here."

"All right, Papa. I'm going now."

A small noise could be heard and then the manager's angry voice. "You listen, girl. Stop sniffing around the bunkhouse and don't sell yourself short for the likes of Luke Clanton. He's only a gunslinger and a poor one at that. He doesn't have two pennies to rub together. I didn't pay money for that fancy school for ladies in Chicago and more money to keep you dressed like that, so you go after the likes of Clanton."

"Leave me alone Papa." She protested and her voice got a higher pitch. "At least Luke is young and good-looking. If you think I'll waste my youth and beauty on the old Mr. Fisher, you're wrong."

"Silly girl, Fisher is rich. You could be a rich

widow and enjoy life as you want."

"And what should I do? Watch in the mirror how my beauty fades away waiting for old Fisher to die? I don't think so." With an audible huff, she ran away.

Then there was silence. The breeze brought in the noxious smell of cigars.

Pierce stepped back and turned away. In the doorway, Aunt Edith placed her finger on her mouth warning him to keep silent and gestured to go into the kitchen. There, she placed some cookies on the table and a mug with tea. Pierce preferred coffee usually, but right now it didn't matter much.

"She is quite something, isn't she?" he said, a hint of yearning in his voice.

Aunt Edith stopped wiping the table and looked at him shaking her head. "She is beautiful, but looks are deceiving. In reality, if you peel off the beauty mask, she is a vain, spoiled woman."

"Ah, but the man who succeeds to tame her..."

The older woman took a seat at the scarred wooden table. "That man could expect a knife in his back at any time."

"Why do you say that? I'm sure she's not so bad."

"I say that because I know her kind. She is that bad. I know because my own sister was like that, so beautiful that men stopped in the street to look at her. But her beauty was only skin deep."

"What happened to her?" Pierce asked with curiosity.

"She was hit by a coach in the street, the day that she was running away to meet her lover, abandoning her husband and her three year old son."

Pierce touched her hand with compassion. "I'm truly sorry. I see you regret her even now and I suppose many years have passed."

Aunt Edith nodded. "I miss her now, like it was yesterday."

"What happened to her husband and son?"

"Rather soon after, the husband married a woman exactly opposite her, a modest, austere woman who raised his son. He married her, for the boy who needed a mother."

"Did he ever think of your sister? Did he regret her?"

She hesitated. "I think he did, but I don't know for sure. Of mutual accord, we had never spoken about her, nor said her name again." She rose from the table. "You are a good man Pierce. Don't fall prey to such a woman. Men are so easily entranced by a pretty face. Life is hard and especially here in the west, a man needs a reliable partner. A helpmate, not a burden."

She paused wanting to say more, but she changed her mind. Waving her hand, she left the kitchen moving slowly.

Pierce stayed there long after his tea had cooled and thought of Aunt Edith's sister and of the beautiful Vanessa Warner. The probability that she would look at him with desire and love was so small that he concluded it was not worth losing sleep over it.

What could he do if at night in his dream, Vanessa's pretty face came again and again?

CHAPTER 8

Early in the morning, Pierce saddled his horse and left for a ride to see the spread. The horse, which had yet to get a proper name, was eager to go.

"You thought I had banished you to pull the buggy from now on, didn't you boy?" Pierce patted him on the neck with affection.

Like Aunt Edith the day before, he marveled at the wide open space and wondered where the boundaries of his brother's ranch were. It was such an exhilarating feeling to ride free and unfettered, one with the horse.

He didn't know for how long he rode, but he decided to go at a slower pace and he veered to the right, riding up a knoll. When he reached the top, he dismounted and feasted his eyes on the view of the valley bellow. Then he blinked amazed at what he saw. Thousands of peacefully grazing cattle dotted the landscape. At first he thought he had accidentally ridden on a neighbor's land. Then he realized he was still on his brother's land. How could that be? If all the cattle belonged to his brother, then Bill's ranch was very prosperous and he wouldn't have agreed so easily to the arrangement Pierce had proposed. Probably Bill had no idea he had so many cattle. His manager had a lucrative operation going on here without Bill being any wiser.

Stunned by what he'd seen, Pierce mounted his horse and slowly guided him through the rocks down the knoll. Then he gave his horse free rein to run. Lost in thought, he didn't pay attention to his surroundings until a whistling sounded behind him, to his right. He tried to turn, but before he understood what was going on, there was a loud hiss and the loop of a lasso tightened around him and he was pulled down from the horse.

He fell to the ground with a jarring thud and the shock of the fall made him see stars. Someone pulled him up roughly from the ground and pushed him forward, while another man hit him with a fist in the face laughing loudly.

He couldn't move or defend himself because his arms were tied down by the lasso. There were three men and their faces were covered by dark bandannas. This didn't matter. He would have recognized them anywhere. They were the three henchmen hired by Warner, the manager, the three that had met him and Aunt Edith the day before.

Now they were laughing and pushing him from one to the other and hitting him until he fell down again. Every inch of his body hurt and he prayed for oblivion. He knew he was close to passing out as the blows came over and over again.

A shot rang out and he knew no more.

He woke up and opened his eyes, then wished he had not. The pain returned and the light from a lamp near his bed hurt his eyes. An old, ugly Indian with a stony face was standing near his bed.

"Mmm... pft...," he tried to speak. His mouth hurt and he checked with his tongue if any teeth were missing. Fortunately, they were all there.

"He's awake," the Indian said.

A tall man in his mid-thirties came closer to the bed and looked at Pierce. "Thank you, Four Fingers. He was lucky you were here today. You're the best doctor out here."

"Hurt." Pierce managed to say.

The tall man nodded. "It's no wonder after taking such a roughing at the hands of Warner's men. They don't like anyone interfering with their business. What I don't understand is why they were masked. You were on their land and from their point of view, you were snooping around, so they had the right to chase you away. Why did they run away when I arrived? Who are you?"

"Pierce... Monroe," Pierce succeeded to say.

Surprise showed on the man's face. "You don't say! Are you a relative of the sheriff?"

"Brother."

"Ah, so you came to visit the ranch and Warner felt threatened."

The observation proved to be so close to the truth, Pierce realized the stranger knew more about the whole story than he did. "Tell me."

"You want to know what is going on at the

ranch," the man guessed. He pushed a chair closer to the bed and took a seat. The old Indian stood near the window with his arms crossed over his chest and the same stony, unreadable face. "I'll tell you. But first answer this, did the sheriff send you to the ranch and how long, if at all after this beating, do you plan to stay?"

"Long," Pierce confirmed, wondering if he'd be able to talk more and explain the deal he had with Bill.

The man did not need any more explanations for the moment. "Good. We need someone honest interested in making this ranch work."

"Tell the boy who you are, John," the Indian said.

"No boy," Pierce protested. For the first time, a smile cracked the old man's face.

"I'm John Gorman," the tall man said. "My land sits between the sheriff's ranch and the Maitland property. Until last year, your brother's land belonged to a man called Crawford and Warner was his right hand. People say a few years ago Crawford had not been a bad man, but his wife died and his sons left back east to study or do other business and Crawford became obsessed with becoming the richest man around and owning more land than anyone. I didn't know him personally because I only moved here last year."

"Bill…" Pierce wanted to say that his brother had been here long before and probably had known Crawford.

"Yes, the sheriff knew him well. So, Crawford started to pressure his neighbors to sell their land to him. Some of the smaller ranches folded first. It's difficult to make a living on a small plot of land. People had no choice and sold their land to Crawford for a small fraction of what it was worth. The ranch I own was a larger one and a target because it was neighboring Crawford's land. The owner, Miller, had a large family and was not very good at managing his ranch. He was willing to sell and move to Colorado where his two older sons were prospecting for gold. But Crawford offered him a pittance, so, Miller was happy when he met me in town, recently arrived and willing to settle and buy land. We agreed on a decent price and right there we wrote the papers, visited the local land office, and transferred the property."

Pierce would have smiled if he could have done it without hurting. "Was Crawford mad?"

"No, he didn't find out immediately and he was busy fighting Maitland, my neighbor to the east. When he saw that Maitland was no push-over like Miller and he would not sell, Crawford tried to chase him away. He hired gunslingers and started to harass Maitland and one night the conflict escalated." A grimace marred John Gorman's handsome face, like a painful memory he didn't relish remembering. "Four Fingers here remembers that night. He is Maitland's man, but visits me from time to time. He's sweet on my cook." He looked affectionately at the old Indian, who mumbled some unintelligible words of denial.

"What happened?" Pierce asked, more interested in the land feuds than the Indian's love life.

"It was right after Christmas and I was having dinner with the Millers. I owned the ranch already, but I told the Millers to take their time packing and leaving. Secretly, I was hoping Miller would teach me the ropes of ranching because I had no experience. After dinner, I left them to enjoy a family evening together and, feeling restless, I went to the barn where my horse was. As any lonely man, I got into the habit of talking to my horse. It was dark outside and far across what was now my land I saw the flicker of light. I went outside and saw a bunch of riders carrying torches. They were at a distance, but still I realized they had no business riding toward Maitland's ranch with torches."

"What did you do?"

"I saddled my horse and rode after them. When I reached Maitland's house, I landed in the middle of a shoot out. I think Crawford wanted to burn the house and force the family to go. He and his men didn't expect full opposition from the family who were not surprised by his arrival and returned fire shot for shot. Crawford's men were caught in the open. Some were hurt, some were hiding behind whatever they could find in the yard. I rode into the opened barn and saw Crawford pull a gun on Maitland, whose own gun was on the ground. I didn't hesitate and I shot Crawford."

"You did? Good." Pierce said. Justice had been done swiftly.

"Warner was not there. He didn't care for Crawford's greed for more and more land, not because he was a better man, but because his interests lay elsewhere. He raised cattle, Crawford's cattle, and most of the profit went into his own pockets. I have no proof, but that's what I think. As long as Crawford was busy feuding with his neighbors, Warner had free hand with the ranching operation."

The story was so interesting that Pierce forgot his pain and tried to get up in a sitting position. A knifing pain told him his ribs were probably broken.

"I bound your ribs, but they are going to hurt for a while and you have to take it easy," the Indian cautioned him, while Gorman helped him by placing another pillow behind his back to support him.

"How did Bill get to own the ranch?" Pierce succeeded to ask, although his mouth was tender making it difficult to speak.

Gorman chuckled. "This is a whole different

story. Crawford's youngest son came to town to avenge his father. He had no interest in the ranch, but he got drunk at the saloon and, because I was there by chance looking for the sheriff, young Crawford tried to shoot me. Drunk as he was, he broke the saloon's large mirror. Tom Wilkes, the saloon owner, asked the sheriff to keep junior Crawford in jail until he paid for the mirror. It was a special order mirror from Denver, or so he claimed. The young man had no money and on top of it, for personal reasons, he wanted to leave town the next morning. When the sheriff explained to him that he couldn't leave until he paid his debt, Crawford junior offered to the sheriff the only valuable thing he possessed, the deed to the ranch. The sheriff had no interest in ranching, but he wanted to help the young man."

"Wow!" Pierce was amazed how easy the ranch had come in his brother's possession while others had to work a lifetime to own such a prime piece of land.

"Because he had not been involved in the attack at Maitland's house, Sheriff Monroe kept Warner to manage the ranch. Neighbors, including me, warned him that Warner is cheating him and there are illegal cattle operations going on at the ranch, including a haven for cattle rustlers, and a place to change brands on livestock. He promised to fire Warner and his men, but events with the last stagecoach to Centennial and the outlaws hiding there in the Medicine Bow Mountains kept him busy. I assume that's why he sent you."

"Yes," Pierce whispered through his bruised lips. For the first time since he had shaken hands with his brother on this deal, he thought that perhaps he bit more than he could chew. His usual optimistic nature and uplifted spirit took a dive and he doubted he could succeed.

But what else could he do? He would die fighting Warner and his henchmen. After seeing the place and listening to the story, he knew for sure that his destiny was here on this land.

CHAPTER 9

Summer nights were usually cold on the high Laramie plateau. But this night was balmy and even a little muggy. Gabe McCarthy sniffed the charged air and hoped a big storm was not going to develop out of this calm and pleasant weather.

He was doing his nightly rounds through town. Bill Monroe, the sheriff was at the office. He was like a bear with a sore paw. He had to go again after the outlaws hiding near Centennial and now he worried about his little brother, although he didn't want to admit that perhaps he'd been too hasty to send him to deal with Warner and his men alone. And to top it all, the Baltimore woman had sent another newspaper with a new episode of the valiant sheriff as a hero, but not one personal word attached to it. If she didn't want him, then she should leave him alone – that was Gabe's opinion. He was glad not to be a fool in love.

He hoped the kid was not in love too. The girl, Gabe was watching as a favor to Pierce, was trouble with a capital letter T. Dressed as a boy, she cleaned the saloon in the morning and cleaned or worked at the millinery shop in the afternoons and evenings. That wouldn't be so bad if she didn't return to the saloon at night. What she did there was a mystery, probably more cleaning for a plate of food from the kitchen, but being there was dangerous even under the disguise of boy clothes.

Gabe stopped in front of the millinery shop and looked at the sign above the entrance, 'Priscilla's World of Fashion', a pretentious name for a hat shop, proof that the owner Miss Priscilla had grand ambitions of her own. In such case, Laramie was not the right town for her. Look at the ridiculous hat in the window. No local woman would be caught dead wearing it. Fashion reigned in the East, but a practical hat was more important here. There were elegant women here too, but not outrageously dramatic except perhaps Cora Lynn, the banker's soon-to-be former wife in search of another rich husband.

His musings on fashion were interrupted when he

saw a light flickering inside the store and heard some noise. He stepped aside. He knew the owner lived upstairs so it was not unusual for Miss Priscilla to work late at night, long after the store was closed. Gabe had no reason to suspect a thief was prowling inside.

The door opened and a man left the store closing the door slowly, careful not to make noise. He looked left and right furtively without seeing Gabe, pulled his hat lower on his head, and crossed the street hurriedly, disappearing at the next corner.

Gabe shook his head in wonder. The respectable Miss Pricilla, proprietor of the World of Fashion, was having an affair with JR Turner, the banker's disgraced nephew. He was the one leaving the store. Gabe recognized him because he was one of the few men in town who wore a fancy top hat, like the gentlemen in the East instead of a plain cowboy hat. Too bad. Miss Priscilla was not only a beautiful woman, but also she was decent.

People said JR had been stealing from the bank for a long time, and his uncle either didn't know – and that was hard to believe – or he chose to ignore the fact. JR had more ambition than stealing; he intended to take over the bank and replace the old banker. After his uncle had returned from the dangerous travel to Centennial with the last stagecoach, he had decided it was time to clean his house and the bank. He filed for divorce from Cora Lynn and fired JR.

The door to the store opened again and Priscilla looked outside.

"He's not worthy of you, Miss Priscilla," Gabe couldn't stop from telling her. Usually, he didn't interfere in other people's lives and he expected the hatmaker to rebuff him and his advice.

To his surprise, she only smiled sadly. "I know, I know. But it's too late now," she said. Then she stepped back inside and closed the door.

A woman of many secrets, Miss Priscilla – Gabe concluded – and what on earth did she mean that it was too late? Not his business. He should go to the saloon to watch over Pierce's cursed girl, dressed as a boy.

A shot rang not far away, in the same direction

the banker's nephew had gone. Gabe pulled his gun out of the holster and ran there. The streets were lighted, but not the side alleys or the spaces between buildings. He stopped at the corner and flush with the building wall, he turned and bent to look into the alley. It was pitch black.

Another shot rang out this time in his direction. He fired back without a clearly defined target. Steps sounded running away and Gabe threw caution to the wind and ran guided by sound. The alley opened into another street where there was some light, but the street was deserted. Gabe stopped uncertain in what direction the shooter had gone.

A moan behind him made him return to the dark alley. His eyes were becoming accustomed to the darkness and he discerned a man on the ground. He approached carefully and kneeled.

"The queen… of spades…," the man on the ground said haltingly, breathing with difficulty.

"Hey, is anybody there?" a man's voice asked from the street.

Gabe turned and saw a man with a house robe

hastily donned over a nightshirt, holding a gas lantern in his hand. The man was hovering there, not daring to enter in the alley. He was no doubt one of the shopkeepers who lived upstairs above his shop. "I'm Deputy Sheriff McCarthy. A man was shot here. Bring the light, please. It's safe. The shooter ran away," he assured the man, who after a moment of hesitation made his way toward Gabe.

When the light from the lantern fell on the shot man's face, Gabe remembered who he was right away. "What do you know, it's the gambler from the saloon."

"Do you know him?" the portly man holding the lantern asked.

"Yeah, I saw him in the saloon gambling. He's not from around here," Gabe explained, his mind working frantically to remember more details about the professional gambler.

"I wonder who killed him?" the shopkeeper said, lifting the lantern higher so the light fell directly on the man on the ground.

Gabe was thinking along the same lines. The

banker's nephew had left a minute or two before Gabe had heard the shot. It might or might not be him. Being a money swindler didn't make him a killer too. "Let's get him to the doctor," he told the shopkeeper.

"Better take him to the undertaker. He's deader than a doornail," the shopkeeper said. Losing interest, he turned to go back home. "His kind always ends like that."

Shot dead in a dark alley. Gabe shivered despite the warm summer night. He had to go to the office to get a horse to carry the dead man to the undertaker. Something twinkled in the darkness. On the front of the man's necktie, there was a stickpin with a winking stone. Gabe took it out and decided not to leave the dead man in the alley after all.

He hoisted him over his shoulder, wincing at the heavy weight and carried him to the lighted street. There he met Timmy, going home late from the train depot. Together they carried the man to the undertaker.

The undertaker grumbled to be awakened so late at night, but he promised to take care of things.

"Are there any relatives of his in town?" he asked after he collected all the possessions found in the dead person's pockets. "No money here. I reckon he'd been robbed," he said with the impassivity of a man who dealt with such situations often.

"No relatives," Gabe answered. "None that I know of. He was just passing through town. I'll take his personal belongings. If any family comes to ask, they are at the Sheriff's Office."

The caretaker nodded. "I bet no one will come."

Gabe felt a shiver of apprehension again. It could have been him instead. A gambler drifting from place to place, with no family and no one to care if he ended up shot dead in a back alley. "I'll pay for his funeral. Make it decent," he heard himself saying.

Back at the office, he found Bill Monroe still there, burning gas to read his Baltimore Sun paper and sighing from time to time.

"Bill, this can't go on any longer. Either go East to ask the fancy lady to marry you or throw away all the papers gathered in your drawer and go on with your life,"

THE YOUNGER BROTHER

Gabe told the sheriff.

Bill narrowed his eyes and looked askance at his deputy. "You're not my mother to tell me what to do. And what got your dander up?"

Gabe took a seat in the other chair and wiped his forehead with his hand. It was not like him to interfere in anyone's life. His own trouble was enough. "A man was shot dead in a back alley. I took him to the undertaker."

"All right. Did you know him? Why did this upset you?" Bill asked not understanding. It was not that Bill was callous or uncaring, but people being shot happened. As sheriff, he dealt with these situations more often than others.

"No, I didn't know him. Not personally. He was a gambler passing through town." Gabe took the dead man's belongings out of his pocket. "This was on him," he said pointing to the stickpin. "It could be glass, but I doubt it. Only a real diamond sparkles like that."

"So? He was a gambler. He must have won it in some game, probably cheating," the sheriff added as an afterthought, not understanding why his deputy was affected by the gambler's death. Then he remembered that Gabe McCarthy had been a gambler too, a real one and acting as one while searching for answers in his activity as a Texas Ranger and later on as a US Marshal.

"I would like you to let me investigate his death," Gabe finally said.

"What is there to investigate? If we know the killer, then we haul him to jail until the judge decides his fate or, if he is a known gunslinger on the run, we go after him. That reminds me that I have to go after the outlaws hiding in the mountains. And now I have to worry about my brother too." He rubbed his eyes, a sign that the valiant sheriff needed spectacles, not that he would admit it. "I was hoping to postpone firing Warner and his hired men for later. Finding out who killed a cheating gambler is not on my priority list. Sorry."

"Don't worry. I'll take care of it and assure some order in town while you go after the outlaws. As for Warner, I think the kid will surprise you by doing exactly what he said. He will get rid of Warner and all the shoddy deals going on at that ranch. He is determined and has guts. He'll do it. Just you wait and see."

"I wish I had your confidence in him, but I'm afraid he'll fail. And if anything bad happens to him, I'll never forgive myself."

CHAPTER 10

Pierce insisted he wanted to return home to the ranch the same day. He liked listening to the friendly rancher, who patched him up after the beating he'd taken at the hands of Warner's men, and he was grateful to the somber Indian, but he had to go back. Otherwise Aunt Edith would be worried and he couldn't abandon her with the likes of Warner. Furthermore, he did not want to give his enemies the satisfaction that they had succeeded to beat him into submission and chase him away. He was no coward.

John Gorman advised him to wait at least until the next day to give his body a little time to heal. "And let me give you one of my most reliable men to stay with you until you feel able to face Warner on your own." It was clear that he didn't believe Pierce was the right man to confront the greedy manager alone.

It was still painful to speak, but Pierce forced the words out. "I appreciate everything you did for me, rescuing me, and binding my broken ribs tight." He nodded his thanks to Four Fingers. "They took me by surprise. Trust me, I can deal with them. No matter how much I'd like the help of another man, I can't accept it." He halted to take a deep breath. "I have to do it on my own. For the deal I made with my brother and for myself."

The rancher looked at him with doubt, wanting to argue with him, but at the same time understanding the younger man's pride and need to assert himself. "Very well," he said, looking at Four Fingers for another idea.

"A man's gotta do what a man's gotta do, alone in this case," the Indian said. "You could loan him the Captain though."

"What a great idea." Gorman went out of the room and whistled. In a minute, he came back followed by a huge German Shepherd dog. The dog sat near his master's foot and looked up with bright intelligent eyes. "This is Captain, my best and loyal friend. He saved me countless of times."

"I can't take your dog," Pierce said.

"Only until you get rid of Warner. I have an

interest in this. I take good care of my cattle and lately I observed there were a few heads missing. I don't have any proof it's Warner or some of the people he's associated with, but who else could it be? I know my other neighbors. Both Maitland and Parker are honest, hard-working men. I can't say the same about Warner."

"I see." Pierce understood that it was much worse than he'd thought. The manager was not only cheating Bill, but was in cahoots with rustlers who stole cattle from other ranchers in the area.

The tall rancher came closer to the bed and, with Four Fingers' aid, Pierce sat up on the bed's edge. The dog came to sniff his hand to get to know him and then sat near the bed.

"I have my doubts about you facing Warner alone," Gorman said. "And stay away from his daughter," he continued advising Pierce.

This surprised Pierce. Had the tall and handsome rancher been hurt by the proud Vanessa? "She's very beautiful."

"She's poison," Gorman spat and because

Pierce's face reflected his thoughts like an open book, he added, "She tried her wiles on me and it didn't work. I could see through her cunning act and also another woman was on my mind all the time." Seeing Pierce opening his mouth to ask questions, he raised his hand. "It's personal and I'm not going to say any more about it. You should avoid Vanessa and not be gullible enough to believe her."

"I will," he promised, although the memory of the beautiful blonde made his heart beat faster.

Unaware of his reluctance, John Gorman continued talking. "Apart from the three gunfighters, Warner has three or four cowboys taking care of the cattle. They are in summer camp and I don't think you saw them at the ranch house. They are not hostile, but you can't rely on them either. After all, they were hired by Warner. He pays them and they take care of his business."

"Perhaps I can convince them to help me," Pierce said.

The rancher shook his head. "No, I don't think so.

They are on the range every day and I'm sure they are aware of the unlawful goings-on there. Cattle brought overnight and brand changed and strangers hiding there and running from the law. First, you'll have to replace these people with your own men. Unfortunately, it's summer and all the men are already hired for the season. Just come to talk to me after a couple of days when you'll feel better. I'll think of something."

Pierce nodded and stood up from the bed with great effort. He had to go back to the ranch. If only he could mount his horse… That reminded him. "I hope my horse found his way back."

John Gorman laughed. "Your horse is right here in my barn enjoying his oats. He saved your life. Four Fingers and I were riding at the boundary of my land when we saw the three masked men and we fired a shot in warning. They ran away and then we saw a riderless horse roaming at a distance. First I thought it was one of the wild mustangs that are often seen around. Then I saw that the horse was saddled and in fact he was not freely roaming, he was returning over and over to the same spot. We went to investigate and found you unconscious on the ground and the horse hovering there near you. Have you raised him from colt?"

"No. I just bought him a few days ago in town."

"Go figure. He's a good horse and he's proven to be loyal to you. Take good care of him. Now let's go before night is upon us."

They helped him mount his horse and accompanied him most of the way home. Pierce was proud of holding up in the saddle, although several times he thought he'd pass out again from pain and weakness.

When the ranch house came into view after a ride that seemed endless to Pierce, they stopped and John Gorman dismounted. After a few more words of advice to Pierce, he kneeled and hugged his dog. Then he mounted up and turning his horse around, both he and the quiet Indian rode back to Gorman's place.

Left alone, Pierce shivered with apprehension and looked at the dog waiting patiently nearby. "Well Captain, it's just you and me now. Let's go face the den of vipers, as they say."

He led his horse on and the dog trotted obediently near him.

He found the ranch house surprisingly quiet. With some difficulty, he dismounted or slid down, holding onto the saddle not to fall, and when he recovered his balance, he led the horse into the barn.

After taking care of his horse, he made his way slowly to the house followed by the dog. It was already dark outside, a beautiful summer night, with crisp, cool air and starry night.

"Well hello, handsome." He heard Vanessa's sultry voice. She was sitting on the porch swing, moving slowly. "Come sit near me." She patted the seat next to her on the swing.

Pierce was exhausted and all he wanted was to find his bed to lay his battered body on a soft mattress. Despite his misgivings and Gorman's advice, the invitation was tempting and he found himself gingerly sitting on the swing near her. After pausing in front of Vanessa, the dog rested at Pierce's foot.

"Where did you find this stray dog? I like dogs,

but Pa won't let him in the house," Vanessa said, bending down to pet Captain, who didn't growl at her. Was he more of a lapdog than the fierce guard dog that the rancher was so fond of?

"I got him from our neighbor, John Gorman," Pierce explained, without giving other details or mentioning that what her Pa wanted was of no consequence to him. His brother owned the house, not Warner.

"Ah, John Gorman, forever in love with the whey-faced Esme Richardson," Vanessa said with scorn in her voice.

His blasted curiosity surfaced. It had gotten Pierce in trouble so many times before. "Who is Esme Richardson?" he asked.

"You are new to the area and don't know. Esme was or is, it's not clear, the sister of our neighbor to the west, Lloyd Richardson. People say she was in love with an outlaw who was killed by a bounty hunter. After that, Esme vanished. The family claimed she moved permanently to Chicago, but the locals say she died of a broken heart and the family wanted to hide the truth, including that she was the outlaw's lover."

"Sad story. But what does it have to do with John Gorman?"

"Gorman was in love with the sad Esme. Some men are like that. They prefer sad, unhappy women attracted by their tragic air, instead of real women, full of life and passion," she commented, with resentment in her voice.

Yes, that was quite a story of misdirected love. He was so deep in thought, that he almost missed her change of subject.

"What about you? Have you given your heart to a lucky woman?"

"No, Miss Vanessa, I have not." He didn't add that in the farm community in Kansas were he lived all his life there were not many choices and men had to go to town or write for mail-order-brides to get married. Love was seldom part of this.

"Hmm." She touched his face. "What happened to your face?"

THE YOUNGER BROTHER

Pierce was hoping the darkness of the night would hide his bruises. A lantern was hanging near the entrance door and gave some light though. "Nothing," he denied. "It must be a shadow from the dim light of the lantern."

"Is that so? Let me see," she whispered seductively, moving closer to him and touching his face.

He knew she was toying with him, but what did it matter? She was so tempting and there were not many women knocking on his door waiting to be kissed. If she was willing, why not? He had only to bend his head to touch his lips to hers. No one would be wiser and no harm done.

He did just that, but in a fraction of a second he saw her eyes. It was not the dreamy face of a woman desiring to be kissed, but the calculating look of a person very much aware of what she was doing and why.

Pierce guessed that Vanessa didn't cozy up to him tonight to please her father. She had her own reasons. She was the kind of woman who needed every man's attention. She needed their admiration and devotion. Apart from vanity, she wanted to be able to manipulate them to her own purposes. Beauty was her weapon and she knew how to use it.

Regretfully, he pulled back.

Sensing his withdrawal, her eyes hardened. "What's the matter? Did you lose your nerve or are you too inexperienced to know what to do with a woman?"

Ah, the gloves were off. Maybe it was better this way. Without answering her deliberately challenging words, Pierce rose from the swing.

"Good night, Miss Vanessa," he said and went inside with his dog. Behind him, he heard a flower pot being smashed on the porch. She had quite a temper.

CHAPTER 11

"Dang!" the sheriff exclaimed slapping the desk with his hand. "The outlaws attacked the train to Rawlins and set fire to the old trading post near Lone Tree Creek. I have to go after them early tomorrow," he said morosely. "I'm sorry to leave you alone to assure the order in town, but it needs to be done."

Deputy Gabe McCarthy set his coffee cup on the table near the window and turned to face the sheriff. "Bill, have you thought that perhaps the people who did this are not the outlaws holed up in the Medicine Bow Mountains, but other wanted men hidden much closer to town, on your own property?"

The sheriff raised an eyebrow in surprise, then shook his head. "Nah, I know the ranchers don't like Warner and I'm aware that he's cheating me of some profit, but he's not bad enough to commit a crime. He was not involved in Crawford's plans to force his neighbors to sell their land to him. Warner only managed the cattle business."

"He was stealing Crawford blind. Like he's doing with you now."

"I know. I'm willing to let it go if he spares me the chore of taking care of the cattle myself."

"Gorman is complaining that some of his cattle are missing. So is Maitland. Let's face it. There are rustlers in the area."

"That doesn't mean Warner is doing it," Bill objected, although he was not very convinced himself.

"Gorman suggested that there might be other unlawful things going on right there on your ranch. He had no proof, but I trust his instincts. You should go to investigate. Instead, you sent your innocent kid brother to deal with the whole nasty situation."

That didn't sit well with the sheriff, who got up and started pacing the room. "Gabe, the kid is in fact twenty-six years old. You and I have dealt with worse people and situations, shoot-outs, for twenty years. We survived on our own at a much younger age. If he wants the ranch, then he can have it, but first, he has to prove that he can take good care of it and fight against everyone that might be a threat."

Gabe bent his head, admitting the sheriff was right. "Fair enough. I still can't help it, but be afraid for the kid. He is so innocent."

"Then it's time he lost his innocence."

Gabe rose and took his hat from the peg. "If Warner proves to be worse than a small crook and the kid loses more than his innocence, could you live with your decision?" He didn't expect an answer. It was just food for thought. He saluted and setting his Stetson low on his brow went outside to do his nightly rounds through town.

'This is what happens when you stay in one place for too long' – he thought – 'you start caring about people and become vulnerable.'

There was loud music and noise at Tom Wilkes' Saloon. It was about what could be expected from such a place of entertainment. Gabe walked closer and looked inside, above the swinging doors.

Women's laughter blended with men's voices. The piano player wiped his forehead and started another lively tune. At two tables, men were engaged in playing cards, totally absorbed in the game, undisturbed by the noise that surrounded them. Behind the bar, Tom Wilkes was serving as bartender tonight and smiled jovially at the cowboys lined there enjoying their drinks. It was a good night and Tom was happy, surveying the room from time to time, making sure that the girls were wandering from one customer to the other, to see that their glasses were full.

A usual night at the saloon. Gabe was ready to walk away, continuing his rounds through town, when one drunken cowboy laughed loudly at what his friend said and slapped his hat on the bar counter. That spilled the whiskey from the glass just set on the bar for a newcomer to drink. The glass rolled and fell off, breaking in pieces on the wooden floor. The man who ordered it, looked down in disbelief, then at the amber liquid trickling down from the counter and finally at the drunken cowboy who'd caused all this and who found this so hilarious that he guffawed again, showing his teeth, yellowed by too much tobacco use.

Smelling trouble, Gabe pushed the swinging

doors open and made his way inside, watching the confrontation between the two men at the bar.

Enraged by the cowboy's laughter, the newcomer grabbed him by the coat and pulled him up. "I'll kill you," he announced through clenched teeth.

It was then that the drunken cowboy awoke from his stupor, and realized he was in trouble. "Hey mister," he squeaked. "I didn't do it on purpose. It was an accident," he protested, trying to get away from the other's strong hold.

Tom Wilkes looked worriedly at the mirror behind him and at the splendid Danae painting above it and knew that the cowboy didn't have two pennies to rub together and he couldn't pay for any damages that a brawl might incur. He intervened decidedly. "Gentlemen, please go fight outside, not in my establishment. Here's another drink on the house to compensate for the spilled one."

The sight of a new glass filled generously with whiskey seemed to appease the newcomer, who let go of the cowboy. Turning to the bar, broken glass crunched under his boots.

"I'll call the boy to clean the broken glass," Tom added, trying to prevent more confrontation in his saloon. "Amos!" he shouted.

Gabe shook his head. Tom was smart, although by the end of the night, he'd have a fight in his saloon for sure. He couldn't prevent it. It went hand in hand with too much drinking and high-spirited cowboys.

But for now the brawl was stopped and Gabe was ready to go. A door to the back quarters, where Tom's office and the kitchen were, opened and a slim boy with a cap on his head came in carrying a pail and a broom. Gabe knew instantly that this was Pierce's friend Amy. What was a girl like her doing here in a saloon among rough men, cleaning the floor? - he wondered, looking at her placing the glass shards in the bucket, and handling the broom around the newcomer who didn't bother to step aside to make her job easier. He was just sitting at the bar sipping his drink.

At some point he extracted from his breast pocket a piece of paper and squinted, trying to read what was written. Amos-Amy with one swipe of her broom cleaned the last of the broken glass, but unfortunately hit the man's elbow with the handle making him drop the paper, that fluttered to the floor.

Like a bull seeing red the man turned to the boy. "You idiot, don't you watch what you're doing? I'll teach you to do better." And raising his hand threateningly, he hit Amy in the face, almost dislodging her cap.

Tom thought to intervene, but figured out that the man with a temper would calm down after he'd take it out on the boy. It was unlikely the boy would fight back so there was no danger of damages.

Gabe had no such qualms though. In fact, his own usually calm temper started to boil when he saw the man striking Amy. "Hold right there, mister. We don't like bullies in this town, men who strike the weaker and the smaller."

It was summer and Gabe's star was pinned visibly to his shirt. The newcomer with a temper, his attention distracted from punishing Amy, considered his odds fighting a sheriff's deputy, but he thought the provocation warranted a good fight. "Who are you to tell me what to do? I don't care that you have that badge. Let's see if you're man enough to fight me." Saying this, his hand went for his gun.

He didn't get to take it out of the holster. In the blink of an eye, Gabe drew his own Colt pointing it at the man. "Get your hands up. Now!"

Around them, the noise died down and people's attention was directed to the two men confronting each other. Even the piano player stopped his music and turned around to look at them. People got out of the line of fire, but didn't leave the saloon.

The newcomer was not drunk, but perhaps not so bright to admit when he was bested. By now, it was clear to all present that the new deputy, hired only a few months ago by the sheriff, was the fastest gun they'd seen around. Clear to all except the newcomer, frustrated by not being able to vent his temper on a hapless victim. He sensed that the deputy, although fast, didn't want to shoot him. That was a weakness, he decided. If you draw, you shoot instantly or you are killed. The deputy was a mealymouth after all. He drew his gun as fast as he could only to have it knocked out of his hand.

"Get out of here now, if you want to do it on your own feet," Gabe advised him.

The man nodded curtly and bent down to take his gun from the floor only to have it shot out of his reach.

"Leave it. You can take it from the Sheriff's Office when you leave town. Go now."

The man turned and left the saloon, disappearing into the night.

"Why didn't you shoot him?" Tom Wilkes asked Gabe. "He drew first. We all saw it. He came here with an itch to start a fight. I know his kind," he said wiping a glass dry and setting it on the counter. He raised the whiskey bottle.

"No, thank you," Gabe covered the empty glass with his hand.

In the commotion that followed, no one saw the boy quietly leaving the saloon taking his pail and broom with him.

Gabe was thinking along the same lines as the saloonkeeper. Why didn't he shoot the man? He had lectured Pierce the same only a few days ago. The man would find another weapon and probably wait for Gabe in a dark corner to take revenge for the humiliation. It was all he needed, another enemy roaming the streets, trying to kill him. Was he becoming too mellow and tired of chasing outlaws and of gunfighting?

"Tom, I want to ask you something. There was a card player from out of town a few days ago…"

The saloon owner paused wiping glasses and looked at Gabe. "The one you played poker with and beat the tarnation out of him. Yes, I remember him. Yesterday was the last time I saw him."

"Do you remember with whom he played cards?"

"Sure. The usual cardplayers, Carson from the Trabing store, Marty Rodgers from the stables, a cowboy who never said his name, but I've seen him quite often lately. He keeps to himself and doesn't brag like other men. And he doesn't make a big deal when he loses. Oh, and that no good of a nephew of the banker, JR Turner.

He stopped by and played a hand or two."

Gabe thanked him and followed by curious looks, he left the saloon.

"Psst, Sheriff," a woman's voice called behind him.

He turned and saw one of the saloon girls, Angel or Lola – he could never remember which one. She was leaning against the post in front of the saloon and smiling coyly at him.

He arched an eyebrow. "I'm a deputy, ma'am, not the sheriff," he corrected her.

She continued to smile, but it didn't reach her eyes. "If you want more details about what happened yesterday, come to my room tomorrow." She looked inside through the swinging doors. "I have to go back to work now." Swishing her red skirt and moving from side to side seductively, she returned to the saloon.

CHAPTER 12

After the saloon girl left, Gabe looked around to be sure no one was lurking in the darkness of the street and then walked around the corner of the building. The side stairs going to the second level were rather rickety. Maybe the saloon keeper thought that given their state of disrepair, in such contrast to the front and the interior, this would discourage any intruder bent on mischief, trying to access the inside unseen.

Gabe had no intention to climb up there. At least not tonight. Under the stairs, he found the door, almost hidden from view. He knocked on it. No one answered. He tried the handle, but it was locked as he suspected.

He came closer and whispered, "Amy, open the door. It's Deputy McCarthy." Again nothing. "Pierce Monroe sent me."

It seemed those were magic words because the door was unlocked and cracked open just an inch. "Are you alone?" she asked.

"Of course."

THE YOUNGER BROTHER

The door opened wider and Gabe entered a tiny space, filled with buckets, brooms, and rags. Near the back wall, there was a narrow cot and a lantern on a peg. Amy pushed the door closed after him and locked it. A wave of claustrophobic nausea threatened Gabe, who was not comfortable in tight spaces.

"Good grief! How can you live in this hole?"

Amy smiled showing surprisingly white teeth. "This hole, as you call it, is my little piece of heaven. Here I can rest, sleep, and dream in relative safety."

It must be cold at night, although it was warm, even stuffy. "How come it's so warm?"

"The kitchen and the stove are on the other side of the wall," she explained.

She was pretty like this, with her hair unbound, falling to the middle of her back. Her face was nice too. A nasty bruise was starting to turn blue on her cheek.

"I'm sorry," he said touching her face.

There was no space to step back, so she bent backwards to avoid his touch. "What do you want?" she asked suspicious of his reasons.

"Pierce told me to watch over you while he is away at the ranch," Gabe told her while keeping his hands to himself. She was skittish. No sense in frightening her.

Again Pierce's name succeeded to alleviate her fears. Gabe almost envied the kid for being able to gain her trust in such a short time.

"Did Pierce tell you that I'm a girl?"

"No," Gabe admitted. If the kid had promised her not to reveal her secret to anyone it was only fair to tell her the truth. "Pierce asked me to watch over his young friend who cleaned at the saloon. I pieced the rest together myself." Seeing the worry on her face, he hastened to add. "I'm not going to tell your secret to any other soul."

She released the breath she was holding. "Thank you. For this and for stopping that man tonight from hitting me again. Tom Wilkes wouldn't have intervened."

"Amy, I was there tonight, but what if I hadn't been? That man was a bully and a brute. Not only he would have beaten you, but your cap would have fallen off and your secret would have been revealed. Do you know how many of the drunken cowboys in the saloon would like to have fun with a young girl?"

Fear returned to her eyes. She was aware of the dangers. "Nah. The cap is pinned tightly on my hair," she braved it out.

"Why? Why do you take this risk every day? I know you work at that fancy hatmaker. Why don't you move away from here and live like the girl you are meant to be?"

Amy bit her lip. "I need the money I get for cleaning the saloon and this place comes for free. Soon I'll have enough to start a new life. I only have to endure this for a little while longer," she said looking at him, hoping he understood.

Gabe took his hat off and ruffled his hair. "Let's see, there must be a better place. The boarding house is too expensive. What about the hatmaker? Doesn't she have a room or a place there, at that fancy store of hers?"

Amy shook her head. "No. Miss Priscilla has two

rooms upstairs where she lives and receives friends, ladies… She likes her privacy. She helped me a lot, teaching me to make hats, but I can't impose on her to take me in. Besides, I like my independence too. I'm no charity case." She raised her chin with pride. "And Miss Priscilla is a milliner, not a hatmaker."

"She makes hats, doesn't she?" He shrugged, making a mental note to talk to the said milliner about the plight of her help. There must be a corner larger than a broom closet for Amy to live decently.

"Besides, she can't pay me enough now. Maybe in a few months after I master the skill and I'm able to make a hat all on my own, maybe then she could pay me more," Amy continued.

"Hmm, there are a lot of places that could hire a cleaner and pay decently, not the pittance that I'm sure Tom Wilkes gives you for the dirty work of cleaning his saloon after a night of drinking and fighting."

"Those places don't want to hire me. Don't you think I already tried?"

Well, she might have tried, but if she inquired

about a job dressed as a ragamuffin young boy, it's no wonder no one hired her. No hotel owner or restaurant manager wanted his customers' rooms searched and their pockets at risk from the cleaning personnel inclined toward pick-pocketing. Gabe couldn't blame them for protecting their business, but he could talk to them.

"It's late now and I have to continue my rounds. But I'll think of something, I promise. Until then, try to stay safe," Gabe said.

"Wait," Amy looked down shyly. "How is Pierce?"

Ah so the kid knew how to charm the ladies, unlike Gabe who was rusty in that department. Gabe was a rough man of the west. He almost blurted out that the kid was in danger at the ranch and Gabe was worried about him too. He refrained just in time. Amy had her own worries, no need to get alarmed about Pierce. "He's managing the sheriff's ranch. Hopefully, if he proves himself, then his brother will sign half the ranch to him. The sheriff has no interest in ranching or living isolated out there."

"Oh, I'm glad for Pierce. I hope it works out for him."

Gabe nodded and turned to go. Then he remembered something and turned back to Amy. Turning around proved a feat in itself in the tight space. "Tell me Amy, which one is Angel's room upstairs?"

Amy bit her lip again, a sign she was in doubt about what to do. "The girls have been nice to me – well, all except Lola, but she is nasty to everyone. I don't want to help create trouble for them of any kind. I hope you understand."

Yes, Gabe understood. Amy depended of the girls' good will. "I'm not asking as a customer with hidden intentions. Angel asked me to come to her if I want information. I do." He waved his hand. "Never mind. I'll find it." He left the small space. Outside, he took a deep breath of air and looked at the vast expanse of inky black sky with a myriad of bright stars and he felt marginally better.

He heard Amy locking the door after him and then he left the alley near the saloon. The streets were nearly deserted at this late hour of the night and Gabe was thinking to return to the office and seek a few hours of sleep in the cell as usual.

His keen vision alerted him to a slight movement ahead, and he stepped back into the darkness of a shaded porch away from the light of a lamppost across the street. It saved his life as a shot rang out and the dust sprayed right in the spot where he'd been a second before. He pulled out his Colt and squinted to see every detail in the street.

"McCarthy, come out you coward and face a real man," a voice rather thin and young sounded.

"Who's talking about being a coward? You, who shot at me while hiding in the dark?" All Gabe's restraint not to fight unless strictly necessary vanished. This person was dangerous, shooting in the streets randomly, without being sure if it was his target or if an innocent person would be shot. Furthermore, his fighter's instincts were arisen as was his personal pride challenged by the stranger's words.

A dark silhouette stepped out from the place

where he was hiding. He had a gun in his hand.

"Is this a challenge to a fair gunfight or are you planning a cold-blooded murder?" Gabe asked before coming out.

The stranger wavered. It meant he had been paid to kill. It was not a senseless gunfight for the title of the fastest gun in the west. Then the stranger's vanity won and he shouted back to Gabe. "Sure. Why not? A gunfight. I heard you are fast. But not as good with as I am. Let's see." Confident, he placed his gun back in the holster, his hand hovering above it, moving his fingers in a nervous dance.

"Save me Lord from idiots who fight in the middle of the night", Gabe muttered and placed his own gun in the holster, stepping out to the middle of the street. Tom Wilkes warning came back to haunt him. This stranger was determined to kill him. If he'd wanted the ephemeral glory of being the best gunfighter, he'd have waited for the middle of the day with a lot of people to witness his performance.

The light was not so strong and Gabe couldn't see

his eyes to anticipate his movements, but it was good enough to see his fingers. Gabe watched, all his attention focused on them. A slight jerk was his warning. It was kill or be killed, as the sheriff said.

A fraction of a second before the other drew his gun, Gabe's own Colt was out and the shots rang in the quiet street. It had been only an instant, but for Gabe, it all happened in slow motion. He tried to shoot the stranger's right shoulder to disable the shooting hand, but at the last moment, the stranger moved in the opposite direction making Gabe's aim dead centered. The stranger fell face down in the middle of the street.

Gabe walked to him and kneeling in the dust, turned him face up. A childish face, completely unknown to him, stared at the starry sky with unseeing eyes.

"I saw it all, mister. He was waiting for you and wanted to shoot you," a middle aged man said, pulling a house robe tightly around him. "Oh, it's you, Deputy." He pointed at the stranger's body. "One of the outlaws you chased in the past, I'm sure. The world is better without him, Lord forgive him."

But Gabe knew it was not an outlaw from his past. It was a completely unknown stranger who'd wanted to kill him. He had known Gabe's name and the way he used to walk on the streets during his nightly rounds.

"Another one, Deputy?" someone asked. Raising his eyes Gabe saw the undertaker. How did he get here so fast? - he wondered. He didn't bother explaining that he had not killed the first dead man he'd brought in the day before, or that this man had been waiting for him. Nodding, he let the undertaker take the dead body away. All of a sudden, he felt tired of fighting and wondered if it would ever end.

CHAPTER 13

After talking to the beautiful Vanessa on the porch, all Pierce wanted was to find his bed and sleep. He was exhausted. But Aunt Edith was waiting for him in the kitchen; she fed him, checked his bruises, and made him tell her the whole story. He did so willingly, enjoying how she fussed over him. His own mother, while tenderhearted and loving Pierce very much, had not dared to show her feelings fearing his severe father would blame her of coddling him.

When he finally went to bed, with Captain settled on the old braided rug at the end of the bed, he slept unturned until the next morning.

Used to farmers' hours, he woke up right before the sunrise, feeling much better. The house was quiet and he led the dog outside in the cool early morning air. After a tour around the house and into the yard, they returned inside where noise from the kitchen showed that Aunt Edith was up and about, preparing breakfast. Leaving Captain with her to be fed some scraps from yesterday's meal, Pierce went to the barn to check on his horse.

He replenished the oats in the bucket and hugged the horse's strong neck, patting the soft dark coat. "I didn't get to thank you for saving my life yesterday, my friend. You're my hero. How would you like to be named Hero?"

The horse bobbed his head up and down and playfully nudged Pierce in the shoulder. Pierce laughed amused by the horse's antics, but his amusement ended suddenly. There was a noise outside, steps running in and out, and the horse stepped back neighing, sensing danger.

Pierce ran out of the stall and smelled smoke. There were several bales of hay near the entrance. Someone had thrown a lighted Lucifer on the one in front and it had started to catch fire.

The animals were becoming agitated and Pierce was in panic, not knowing how to save them. He ran back to the stall and grabbed an almost full bucket of water. He poured it over the bale on fire and it extinguished somewhat. Not entirely though. It was still smoldering, threatening to start burning again.

THE YOUNGER BROTHER

Pierce ran into another stall and grabbed another bucket, this one only half full. He came back to the fire. He heard the noise of someone closing the barn doors and placing the bar across on the outside.

He was horrified. He knew that Warner and his men wanted to chase him away, but to endanger the animals was inexcusable no matter how reckless the lowlife was. He was enraged and this gave him an unusual strength and determination. He forced himself to be calm and think.

There were some tools placed carelessly along the wall. Pierce picked up the fork.

Between the two large doors of the barn, there was a narrow space where he could see the light. He stuck the fork sideways there, right under the bar and forced it forward, wiggling it to enlarge the crack between the doors. Then he pushed it up with all the force he could muster. The bar budged, but not enough to open.

Desperate now, Pierce looked back at the hay. It was smoldering, but the smoke was thicker. Trying again, Pierce added a hit with his knee up. Again and again until the bar was raised enough that he could push the barn door open.

Outside, the three cowboys were laughing, as if killing the animals was a good joke. They made no effort to hide that they had set fire to the hay. But Pierce paid no attention to them. He ran to the trough and filled the bucket with water. Then returned to the barn and poured it over the burning hay. He repeated this until he was convinced the fire was entirely out. Only then did he stop in front of them facing each one in turn. They were smirking at him.

"Did you wet your pants farmer boy?" the one closest to him asked.

"You could have put out the fire that way," another said, and that sent them all into another round of laughter.

Pushed beyond his limits, Pierce looked at the first one and struck him hard in the face. He'd wanted to inquire who was the one to set the fire, but now he didn't really care. They were all guilty.

"You might have a bone to pick with me for whatever warped reason, but don't take it out on women or animals. How dumb can you all be to burn a barn full of animals just to scare me?" Pierce was not finished pouring out all his outrage, but the man in front of him didn't take kindly to be hit by one he considered a weakling and an easy victim to be picked on.

The corner of the man's eye started twitching nervously and he growled, "No one hits me without being dead the next moment. You, farmer boy are as good as meeting your Maker." He pulled from his belt a nasty looking knife and waved him in front of Pierce.

"Wait!" a woman's voice cried from the porch. Anyone else would have been ignored by the fighting man in the fever of getting to his target. But Vanessa had a way of getting herself noticed. "I like a good fight between two able men." She smiled maliciously. "Let's make it more interesting by equaling the odds." Saying this, she threw a long knife with a thin blade at Pierce's feet.

The man with a knife looked like he intended to

protest, but the leader of the three, the one called Luke, nodded in agreement. "Miss Vanessa is right. Let no one be able to say that this was not a fair fight." The veiled reminder that their intended victim was the sheriff's brother was enough to quiet any protests.

Pierce took off his coat and twisted it around his left arm. Then he picked the knife from the ground. He was still angry over the fire set on purpose in the barn. These men were thoughtless and cruel. While Pierce himself was a peaceful man, who avoided confrontation, he was aware that reasoning with Warner was impossible and getting rid of these people was difficult. He'd hoped to make his brother's ranch free of any crooked characters in a nonviolent way. It seemed this was not possible. So, there had to be a fight. There was no other choice.

The man was the first who struck hard forward, sure that his knife would find the target. To his surprise, he found only air. His opponent was quite nimble on his feet and had stepped aside.

After a few strikes and parries on both sides, it

became clear to the men that what they thought would be another unequal fight in which their friend would toy with a hapless victim to their amusement before finishing him off, was not going to happen. On the contrary, the farmer boy from Kansas showed a marked ability to move around, to avoid being cut and because he didn't strike their man a direct cut, it looked like he was the one toying with an increasingly enraged man, who was breathing harder, desperate of his own inability to best the other.

Nope, it was not going as they hoped at all. Attracted by the commotion in the yard, even Warner came out to see what was happening. Puffing his ever present cigar, he watched the fight with an unreadable expression.

Exasperated by his man's incompetence, the leader came closer and stuck out his own foot to trip Pierce.

A shot rang from the porch. Aunt Edith carrying the old Winchester rifle from above the mantel shook it at them. "No tricks. As Miss Vanessa said, it should be a fair fight. Next time, I won't shoot in the air. The one who interferes will be my target. And trust me, boys, I won many prizes for my shooting prowess."

Good thing she didn't add that it was at country fairs for shooting the moving turkey and not for being another Annie Oakley.

Pierce's opponent, tired and frustrated, was increasingly ineffectual getting at his aim. He jumped forward, placing all his body weight behind the strike. Pierce feinted to his right, parried and leaned to the left. The whole body movement brought the other one right where Pierce's armed hand was. Maybe Pierce's intention had never been to strike the man deadly no matter how angry he'd been, but as it happened in such fights, intentional or not, the man was struck dead in the chest.

He looked at the knife handle protruding from his chest in disbelief, rolled his eyes backwards and fell facedown to the ground.

There was a long moment of silence in the yard, the men stunned by what happened. If at first they had to admit, Pierce was no easy victim for their friend, still they didn't imagine that the fight would end with their man's defeat and death.

It was not supposed to be this way. Didn't Warner say that the sheriff was too busy chasing outlaws and not interested in what happened on his ranch and his brother was just a young farmer boy, easily scared away from their business?

The silence was interrupted by Aunt Edith. "Pierce come inside and let me take care of that wound." His left arm, the one he parried with, had a cut high just bellow the shoulder. "And you," she addressed the other men, "place the body in the wagon and take him to town to the undertaker to have a proper burial like a Christian, regardless of his sins."

Later, in the warm kitchen, Pierce let Aunt Edith clean his wound and tried to breathe gingerly as his ribs were aching again despite Four Fingers' tight bind. All the moving, feinting, and parrying had probably dislodged them again. Not to mention carrying buckets of water to the barn.

"I didn't mean to kill him, Aunt Edith," he said, his heart heavy.

"You had no choice. He wanted to kill you." Aunt Edith said simply, ministering to his wound. She stopped and looked at him. "Sometimes you can't help it. And it's not going to be easy emptying the ranch of their kind. And I'm not talking only about Warner and the three, now two, men he hired. There are others who bring their unlawful business to this place where they feel free to do what they want. No, it's not going to be easy to instate order here. Especially if you insist to do it alone, without anyone's help." She shook her finger at him. "You should have accepted at least your neighbor's help. It was his interest too to get rid of vermin."

Pierce smiled sadly. "I couldn't. It's my fight. And this was the deal I made with Bill."

"Pshaw, deal," she scoffed. "If your brother doesn't want this ranch, why leave it to the mercy of the likes of Warner and not to you?"

"He wants me to prove myself able to take care of it."

"Nonsense. You're family and Warner proved himself to be a crook." She shook her head. "Now, I tried to clean this wound the best I could, but I think we should go to town to see the doctor before it becomes putrid."

"Nah. I cut myself countless times when I worked on the farm and in the end the wounds heal," he answered more worried about his ribs and the restraint in movement they caused him.

CHAPTER 14

It was close to midnight when Gabe returned to the saloon. There were still customers inside and some diehard gamblers. The piano player was continuing his duty, albeit in a slower rhythm.

Gabe looked inside and saw two of the girls, one looking bored behind the card players who paid her no attention and the other enticing a cowboy at the bar to have another drink he obviously didn't need, considering the precarious way he was waving, unsteady on his feet. The one called Angel was not there.

It was what he wanted to know, so Gabe turned around the corner of the building and stopped again in front of the same rickety stairs. This time he climbed up carefully one rotten wood step at a time, afraid to make noise and create a commotion at that late hour, in case one of the steps broke under his weight. It was tricky to go up in the dark, but he succeeded and to his surprise found the door at the top unlocked.

Once inside, he had to figure out which one was

Angel's room. He couldn't blame Amy for not giving him this information. Randomly, he opened a door on the right of the hallway. In bed, an older man was snoring loudly. Sitting on the edge of the bed one of the saloon girls, scantily dressed was smoking.

"Angel," Gabe whispered the question-like name.

"Next door on the left," the girl answered in a loud voice that would have awakened a normal person, but not the old man in the bed. She inclined her head in that direction.

Gabe muttered his thanks and closing the door quietly went to the door she indicated. This time he knocked before trying to open the door. The room was lighted by a gas lantern and Angel was sitting on a chair in front of the dresser, combing her hair, unnaturally colored in bright red.

Relieved to see that she was alone, Gabe entered and closed the door behind him.

She assumed a flirtatious pose, with her legs crossed, making her robe slightly open and her foot clad in an elegant heeled house slipper swinging back and forth. "Ah, you finally came, handsome?"

"Cut the play," he answered rebuffing her. "I came because you offered some information and I need it. That's all."

She wrinkled her nose disappointed. "Alas, nothing is for free in this world."

"Now, we understand each other," Gabe said. "If your information is more than what I already know, I'm ready to pay." He touched his pocket suggestively.

"It is, it is," she hastened to assure him. "You men think the saloon girls are just decorations for your entertainment. You forget that we have eyes and ears, to see and hear and a brain to put two and two together."

"I believe you. Let's hear it." Impatient, Gabe interrupted her.

Angel made a moue, meant to be an attractive pout. "Very well. What you don't know is that there was another man at the card table briefly that night."

Gabe sighed, wondering if he had wasted his night coming here. "I know that. It was JR Turner, the banker's nephew."

"The handsome, smooth-talking JR, who's involved one way or another in all the shady deals in this town. Yes, he was there. But I'm not talking about him. There was another one, not playing, just hulking nearby and at one point talking to the professional gambler."

All right, this piece of information was news to Gabe. "A deal went wrong. That's why he shot the gambler," He reasoned with loud voice.

Angel blinked. "Someone killed the gambler?"

"Yesterday evening, after he left the saloon. Weren't you talking about what happened yesterday?"

"No, I was talking about what happened a few days ago when your young friend, the sheriff's brother was cleaned of his money by the gambler and you had to intervene and gave a lesson to the gambler of both card playing and gunfighting. Weren't you asking about that?"

Frankly he wasn't, but now it made sense that there must by a connection between these events. "They are related somewhat."

"Of course they are. The man paid the gambler to

ruin that naïve kid."

"That's absurd. The kid had just arrived from Kansas. Nobody here knew him, not enough to hold a grudge and want him ruined."

Angel nodded. "True, but many know his brother, the sheriff, and I don't have to tell you how many hold a grudge against him."

Yes, what she said made sense. Many people in trouble with the law, that the sheriff had hauled to jail, could come back later, even years later, to get revenge. Bill Monroe had made a lot of enemies through the years. "Did you see that man again here?"

Angel nodded. "Of course. He comes to the saloon almost every night."

Gabe looked at her. She knew that man well. "Do you know his name?"

She nodded again, raising her eyebrow. Ah, yes, she was willing to tell more for money. Gabe searched his pockets. A noise at the window made him raise his eyes. It was a warm summer night. The window was open and the sheer curtain was fluttering in the slight breeze coming from outside. Across the street from the saloon, there was a lamppost and he saw a shadow of a silhouette in the flickering gaslight.

Instinct, honed by years of dangerous living, made Gabe grab Angel's hand and pull her to the floor. The mirror above the dresser, where she was looking combing her hair, shattered in pieces by a well aimed bullet. Gabe drew his own gun and fired in the direction where the shadow stood on the lower level roof outside the window.

Gabe ran after him out the window on the roof, but he could not see anyone and he knew it was pointless to run after a ghost in the dark. Sighing in frustration, he returned into the girl's room, stepping back through the window.

Angel was still there, prostrate on the floor where he'd left her. At first, Gabe was afraid she'd been shot too. "Are you all right?" he asked her.

"Yes, I am," she answered, accepting his hand to help her get up from the floor. She was still shocked and almost sat on the chair covered in mirror shards. Gabe stopped her and guided her to the bed.

"Angel, can you tell me his name?"

She looked at him like in trance, without understanding. "His name? What name?"

"The name of the man you saw in the saloon. The one we talked about." Gabe searched his pockets again. "I'll pay you." He pulled out several bills.

She raised her hand up to reject the money. "I don't know any name."

"You said you have information. You told me." Gabe was getting exasperated. He understood fear was a great motivator, but he didn't expect her to do such an about-face.

She produced a laugh that sounded more like a mewling, sad and scared. "It was all a joke. I was vexed by your rejection and I wanted to attract you somehow. There was no man. Forget the entire story."

Gabe sensed that there was no way to get any more information out of her. Not tonight anyhow. There was nothing more he could do. He touched his hat in salute. "I guess the man who shot at you was also a joke.

If you told me the truth, then I could protect you better."

"No one can protect me, Deputy. No one ever did. Why do you suppose I landed in a saloon? Because I like it here?"

"You take care, Miss Angel."

Gabe left the room, made his way along the hallway, and exited at the top of the rickety stairs. He looked down into the side alley, but everything was quiet and unmoving. It was one of those nights when nothing went right. Of course, he could have ended up shot dead in the street by an ambitious youngster without brains.

Slowly, he descended the stairs.

When he got to the bottom, on the ground level, he heard the door under the stairs crack open.

"Deputy?"

"Yes, Amy. Aren't you sleeping?"

"How can I sleep when you make so much noise, up the stairs, down the stairs. Not to mention the other people that follow you around," she whispered.

The notion that Amy's hiding place could be discovered by a villain with killing on his mind, made his blood freeze.

"I saw him," she continued. "Not well, but the moonlight fell right there at the bottom of the railings. He has a hideous scar on his left hand. Like branded with a fireplace poker."

"How do you know he's the one I'm looking for?" Gabe asked thinking of other characters visiting Tom Wilkes' girls after midnight.

"He was the one all right. He didn't get inside, but crawled along the roof to the other side of the building. Good night, Deputy."

The door closed with an audible click of the lock being turned on.

The next morning, the sheriff dismissed all Gabe's fears as a product of his fancy imagination. No one had any ax to grind with him and if they had, they'd come to confront him directly. The gambler had been shot either by a robber or by mistake. And that was that. Oh, and the idiotic youngster challenging Gabe to a gunfight, yes, that was somewhat worrisome as the sheriff didn't want his town changed into an O. K. Corral scene. For the moment however, all was quiet. No reason to worry unduly.

Then the sheriff left again to chase the outlaws hiding in the Medicine Bow Mountains, leaving Gabe in charge of keeping peace in town and solving whatever other emergency situations might arise.

Gabe knew the sheriff was not completely unconcerned, but he tended to focus on what he considered a priority and getting rid of the outlaws was his number one interest, especially because he knew he could rely on Gabe to enforce the law in town.

Gabe wondered how the kid was managing at the ranch. For a moment, he considered riding there to see for himself. Then he discarded the idea. There was too much going on in town right now. He hoped the kid was at least keeping himself alive.

And just like that, Gabe was overcome by a strong longing of being alone on the road with no other care than himself and his horse and where his next meal might be.

CHAPTER 15

Next morning when he woke up, Pierce saw a fierce looking Indian at his window. He got up surprised and the Indian made a scary face at him. Laughing, Pierce opened the window.

"Good morning to you too," he said.

"How come you're not afraid of me," the Indian asked disappointed.

"I looked at Captain. Not only was he not growling, but also he was wagging his tail happily. I figured he must know you."

"Yeah, he does. I'm Tom Bald Eagle, Four Fingers' cousin."

"Are you working for Maitland too?" Pierce asked while he was getting dressed fast.

"No, I'm only helping from time to time. John Gorman sent me to tell you that he descended on the camp out on the Monroe land and he caught the three cowboys there changing the cattle brand from Diamond G into Bar M. They were the cattle missing from his ranch. He and his men are taking the three men to the sheriff."

"Let me saddle my horse and we'll ride there together."

Pierce went to the kitchen and told Aunt Edith where he was going and snatched two of the hot biscuits from the plate before leaving.

They found John Gorman and four of his men rounding up some of the cattle. Not a small feat in the ocean of hundreds, perhaps more than a thousand cattle grazing in the valley.

The dog, Captain, ran to his master jumping around with joy to see him again. Gorman hugged his dog and turned to talk to Pierce. He was mad as a hornet. "Look, I found eighteen cattle of mine, three of Maitland's, two of Parker's. The brand has been changed, but I could see the real one when I looked closely. There are more probably. Doesn't the sheriff care what is going on at his ranch? Really Pierce, I'm at the end of my patience. And so is Maitland. It's like Bill Monroe is focused only on chasing after the outlaws hiding in the mountains. He's a good sheriff, but I warned him twice that cattle are missing and the culprits are hiding here on his own ranch. But does he care? No." The rancher took his hat off and raked his blond hair in frustration. "If he won't do anything, then we will. Look, I caught those three men rebranding my cattle. They are Warner's hirelings."

Pierce turned in the saddle. Three sullen men were waiting to the side under the watch of one of Gorman's men who held his Winchester on them. It was a volatile situation and it was a miracle a range gunfight didn't erupt. Perhaps the changes Pierce intended to make should start here. Before he would have to forcibly remove Warner from the ranch, he could get rid of his men.

"Look," Gorman wanted to show him. "You can see the Diamond G brand here. The rebranding was a shoddy business. They had no idea how to do it properly."

"I believe you. Whatever cattle you think are yours or they belong to the other ranchers, feel free to take them back," Pierce answered.

One of the three cowboys hired by Warner threw his hat to the ground in anger. "Hey mister, who do you think you are? Mister Warner will have your head for taking his cattle away."

The man who spoke was the oldest of the three and the one who assumed the leadership of the group. Pierce dismounted and approached him. "The name is Pierce Monroe. My brother is the owner of this ranch. Whatever unlawful business is going on here stops now. You three, take your belongings and go. You're fired. If Mr. Gorman wants to take you to town, go and explain to the judge why you were changing the brands of his cattle."

"You can't fire us," he protested. "We were hired by Mr. Warner. We answer to him."

"Warner is not in charge here any longer. You can go to him wherever he's going. But you are not welcome on my brother's land."

"You talk mighty strongly for one so young. Look around you. There are over a thousand cattle here.

Who will take care for them if we go? It's summer and the peak of the working season. All the available men had been hired already. You'll find no one to work for you," he sneered contemptuously, certain that he had the advantage.

"I'll manage. That's not your problem, is it? You'd better worry about what you'll answer to the judge," Pierce answered with a confidence he didn't feel. He was not naïve not to see that without help, he alone couldn't work that many cattle or take most of them to Kansas City to sell. Perhaps his neighbors would be willing to lend a hired man now and again to help him.

The younger one of the three men stepped forward twisting his hat between his hands. He was not much older than Pierce himself, maybe even younger. "Please mister, I can't leave. I have to work to send money home. I'll do what you say. I'm a hard worker."

He seemed honest, with his clear blue eyes and freckled face, and Pierce wavered, wondering if perhaps he could keep just this one from Warner's men. He could use the help that was for sure.

THE YOUNGER BROTHER

He was watching the young man pondering what to do and saw how he turned from time to time, looking furtively at the chuck wagon. The cover over the wagon fluttered in a corner or maybe it was being lifted. This saved his life. He threw himself to the ground just when he heard a shot and the young man crying, "No, Sam, don't."

Pierce rolled on the ground and drawing out his gun, he shot just where he'd seen the wagon cover move. A cry of distress showed that his bullet had hit the target.

Heedless of the danger, the young man ran to the wagon. The other two tried to run, but where? In the chaos that followed, Gorman's man warned them he'd shoot to kill the next who moved.

Gorman galloped to see what was going on. "Stop shooting or we'll create a stampede and we'll all be trampled. This is a big herd." He looked at the chuck wagon where the youngster was wailing, then at Pierce who stood up and was dusting off his clothes. "What is going on?"

"I'm not sure, but I'm going to find out," Pierce

answered and walked to the chuck wagon. Meanwhile, Gorman's man explained to the rancher that someone was hiding in the wagon and tried to shoot Pierce.

Pierce vaulted up in the wagon seat and pulled the cover aside. The young man was holding a wounded man in his arms and was continuing to sob and cry. "You killed Sam. You killed my brother."

Gently, Pierce pried his hands apart from the man and checked him over. "He's not dead. I just winged him a little," he said grabbing the man's gun from his unresisting hands. "But, he will be dead soon if you don't take him to town to be seen by the doctor. His old leg wound had turned putrid." Even so, he doubted the doctor could perform miracles and this man's wound was badly infected. It smelled so bad, Pierce almost gagged.

He looked around for other weapons, but found nothing.

"He needs a doctor now. Do you understand? You are doing him no favors by hiding him here. Who shot him?" he asked, although the young man was too lost in his own fear and worry for his brother to answer.

An insane thought and flashes of images crossed Pierce's mind. He guessed the answer. "He was one of the train robbers, wasn't he?" No one answered and he jumped down from the wagon.

John Gorman came closer. "Who's inside?" he asked keeping his own hand on the gun, ready for any surprise.

"His brother. He's been shot badly in the leg and he needs a doctor now. Even so, I'm afraid it might be too late. The wound turned putrid."

The rancher nodded and turned to give orders to his men. In short time, the wounded man was up on a horse with his brother behind him, supporting him. The fight had gone out of the young man. He was obeying automatically what he was told to do. The other two protested, but mounted their horses and two of Gorman's men watched over them and led them on the way to town.

"Do you think he'll survive?" Pierce asked the rancher as they both looked after the departing group.

"Who? The wounded man? Probably not. That

was a nasty-looking wound. I wonder how he got it?"

"He was shot by a marshal while he was robbing the train," Pierce answered.

John Gorman looked at him in surprise. "How do you know? Oh, you've been there," he guessed. "Why didn't you say this before?"

"If he'll survive, I figure the sheriff or the deputy will know him from the Wanted posters. If not, it doesn't matter." He turned back to look at the cattle grazing peacefully around them. "We'll have to check them out to see which one belongs to what ranch. I'm not an idiot, I realize there is a lot of work and I need to hire new people. However, I'm glad to be rid of these men. Maybe they were not entirely rotten, but I was not comfortable keeping them on because they were hired by Warner."

John Gorman snorted loudly. "Come on. They knew what changing the brand meant. It was theft and they were aware of it. As for help, unfortunately, what that man said was true. It is the peak of the working season and the hard-working cowboys have been hired. No rancher can spare a hand." He scratched his head, hmm-ed some more, and looked at his remaining men. "I have an idea, the only one I can think of. I'm not sure you'll like it…."

"Oh, I'll like it, I assure you," Pierce interrupted him. "It's not like I have many choices." Or money, he ended the phrase in his mind. His brother hadn't given him any funds and there was no money in the house. He'd looked in the ledgers, but there was no accounting done in more than a year, probably right before Bill had bought the ranch. The money from the ranch had filled Warner's personal wallet or bank account. The same with the ledgers. If there were any, they were kept secretly by the manager. And no wonder with all the unlawful operations going on here.

Anyhow, Pierce had his own money from selling the Kansas farm and mentally he sent a thank you to Deputy Gabe McCarthy, who'd helped recoup his money from the cheating card gambler.

"Wait till you hear. You could ask Tom Bald Eagle to come with a few of his relatives to help you." Gorman said looking at the Indian who was riding among the cattle checking them.

"Isn't he working for you?"

"Sometimes, when he feels like it. Tom is his own man. He'll help, if he wants to."

"How come no one hired him?" Pierce persisted asking.

"There are not many people who would hire Indians and not many Indians willing to work for ranchers. There is distrust on both sides. We'll adjust our way of thinking, but it takes time."

When Pierce talked to Tom Bald Eagle, the Indian agreed readily to bring some men to help him for the summer.

"Why?" Pierce asked curious.

A ghost of a smile crossed the Indian's somber face. "You shared your biscuit with me." He nodded. "It was the best biscuit I've had in a long time," he added.

CHAPTER 16

"You can rot in jail for all I care," Deputy Gabe McCarthy told the three protesting cowboys and locked the cell door after them. "The judge will decide your fate for changing cattle brands." They'd been brought to the Sheriff's Office this morning by two of John Gorman's men. A fourth man, with an infected old wound and barely alive, was left at the doctor's office.

Gabe threw the keys to Jeremiah, a young man, not very bright, but willing to help because his dream was to be a sheriff's deputy and he admired Bill Monroe greatly. "I have to go to see the wounded man. Maybe I can identify him. I am leaving you in charge of the office. You are not to open the cell door for any reason and no matter who demands their release with a sob story, don't do it. Do you understand me, Jeremiah?"

"Yes, sir, Deputy… of course. No release, for no reason." He scratched his head. "Or was it no open door for…?"

"Oh, you'd better give me the keys," Gabe said

losing his patience. He grabbed the keys back from him and taking his hat, he was ready to go. "Come and find me if there is any emergency," he said leaving the office.

A sign with faded paint, Alfred Pendergast, MD. hung above the entrance at the doctor's office. Despite his unassuming figure – he was a short, jovial man – Pendergast was a very good doctor and had saved many lives in the two years since he'd moved to town.

Just inside, Gabe met the pastor. He took his hat off. "Is the man dead?"

The pastor looked at him confused. "What? Oh, no, no one died. I came for the doctor, 'cause my wife is having our child. The seventh one," he clarified.

Having seven children to take care of could explain why the pastor looked frazzled. Gabe had trouble just taking care of himself. A wife and seven children seemed beyond his abilities.

The doctor came in the doorway wiping his hands. "I did the best I could. The rest is in the hands of the good Lord. The man is still unconscious." He saw Gabe and smiled. "Deputy, he's not well enough for you to take him away."

"Can I look at him?"

"Sure. He's here on the cot. I doubt you can get any answers from him. As I said, he's unconscious. He might recover or not. There's half a chance he might. Even if he is lucky enough to survive, it will be a long recovery."

Gabe entered the office and wrinkled his nose at the septic smell of the room. The man lying there had a cadaveric pallor and only a slight movement of his chest showed he was still alive. Nevertheless, Gabe recognized him immediately from the Wanted posters. He was without a doubt the train robber that had escaped from the two marshals. He was not going away from here, not anytime soon, even if he was lucky, as the doctor had said.

Lifting his bandanna to cover his nose, Gabe left the room. "Could you please let me know if he recovers, Doctor?"

"Sure. I'm leaving to assist the pastor's wife, but my wife will watch over him."

Gabe nodded to the tall, sour looking woman who worked with the doctor as his nurse and couldn't imagine a better guardian for the train robber. "Ma'am."

He hastened to leave the doctor's office before his stomach turned. The jail keys jingled in his pocket and he knew that he had to return to the office. The summer breeze and the air outside were a welcome change, even if a little dusty when horsemen rode along the streets.

He decided to walk a little longer. Two men were raising a tall post for the electric wire and the lamp that would provide light to this street. Laramie was one of the first small towns west of the Mississippi to have an electric plant, built just two years ago in 1886. Close to the twentieth century, the town was moving along into a modern era.

His steps took Gabe in front of the milliner's shop with its flamboyant hat in the window, adorned with silk flowers and feathers. Ridiculous, Gabe thought. Who would wear such a confection on her head?

Nevertheless, he had business to talk to the

owner. He entered and the bell above the entrance door pealed. The store was empty of customers, but hearing the bell, Miss Priscilla came from the room in the back to welcome him with a professional smile plastered on her face.

When she saw him, she raised her eyebrow at him in a mute question. No wonder. What could a bachelor deputy want from a shop that catered exclusively to women?

"Good morning, Ma'am," Gabe said politely, taking off his hat.

"What can I do for you, Deputy?" the shopkeeper asked and self-consciously she tucked a wayward curl behind her ear.

Ah, so she remembered their encounter from the other night. What had she said when he'd warned her that JR Turner, the banker's nephew, was not worthy? That it was too late for her. What did that mean? Perhaps she was caught in the oldest trap a woman could be and she was with child.

It was not Gabe's business. He was here on an

entirely different mission. He opened his mouth to speak when he heard her ask, "Can I offer you a suggestion?"

"A suggestion?" he echoed.

"Yes. A suggestion about what hat to buy to the woman who owns your heart," she answered.

He stepped back and almost crossed himself. "No woman owns my heart, ma'am." And no one ever would, he added mentally. "I came to you to talk about a different issue. It's about Amy."

"Amy?" she asked cautiously, not knowing how much he knew about her helper and unwilling to reveal too much.

"Look, I know she's a girl dressed like a boy. She is in danger all the time working at the saloon. I understand Tom Wilkes' girls are helping her, but the danger is there. Two days ago, a drunken bully slapped her and the other night someone shot inside one of the rooms. It is not safe for her to stay there. I'm trying to find a different place for her to live."

The hatmaker measured him with suspicion. "What's your interest in this?"

He hesitated before answering. "It's complicated. A friend of mine, a young man, asked me to watch over her because she might be in danger."

"Why couldn't he do it himself?"

"He lives on a nearby ranch, not in town. Anyhow, doing what he asked, I realized just how much danger she's in. I know she works for you too. Can't you help her? This is what I wanted to ask you. She lives at the saloon in a tiny closet under the stairs, not larger than a mousehole."

"I didn't know…"

"Can't you take her in? Don't you have a small room here? Or at least a similar closet here? That would be an improvement if she could dress as a young lady and not have to work and live at the saloon."

Miss Priscilla looked at him with her cornflower blue eyes and bit her plump lip thinking. "I don't have much space myself. There are two rooms above the store where I live. One is my bedroom, the other the living room and everything else including my kitchen. Downstairs behind the main room of the store, there is a small space where I work."

"No closet?" he asked.

She bit her lip again and his eyes went there. "There is a small one, but it's not livable and anyhow…" She paused in doubt if she should give him more details. "A friend is temporary using it to store some of his belongings before he finds permanent lodging."

Gabe did a double take at her words and paid more attention. Was she talking about the banker's nephew, who had been fired from the bank by his uncle and forced to leave the banker's mansion? He smiled charmingly at the pretty hatmaker. "Could I see this space, Miss Priscilla?"

She thought about it, then waved her hand dismissively. "It's not necessary. What you told me convinced me that Amy needs help. I'll take her in, even if I don't have a spare room. She'll bunk with me. This is only temporary, you understand. It can't be permanent. Both Amy and I need a personal space to live. However, she can come to live with me for the moment."

Gabe bowed to her. "Thank you, Miss Priscilla.

This is very generous of you. And you're right about being only for a while until she finds a second job somewhere that comes with a room. I'll talk to the hotel. If you make her presentable, then I bet they'll hire her." Now he should say Good-bye and leave. But his lawman's sense told him that something was wrong. He didn't want to offend or force this nice woman to do anything against her will, but how could he explain?

She saw him undecided and asked him, "What is it, Deputy?"

"I hate to impose on you Miss Priscilla, especially after you've been so nice and offered to house Amy."

"But?"

"I still would like to see that small space."

She straightened her spine. "Of course, as deputy sheriff, you can."

"No. I don't want to force you to open that closet if you don't want."

"Come," she said simply pointing to the back of the store. "I don't know what you hope to find, but there are only a trunk and two portmanteaus with clothes, books."

"Do they belong to JR Turner?"

She nodded. "Yes, they do. I know he's not the best or the most honest person, but he's not as bad as people tried to picture him after he had that fall out with his uncle."

He stopped her before getting to the closed door in the back. "Miss Priscilla, I don't listen to gossip. That night, when JR Turner left your place, a man was killed around the corner from here. I have no proof that it was JR and I am not implying that he was, but I have to investigate this crime from all angles."

She sucked in her breath. "Surely, you don't think it was JR. He is a gentleman."

Gabe could have told her about many gentlemen who had committed heinous crimes. A monster can hide in a simple man or in a gentleman just as well. But he held his silence.

She opened the door. It was indeed a narrow, long space, probably used as a tiny kitchen by a previous owner. There was a rack with hats in various stages of decoration, a trunk in the corner and two portmanteaus. The trunk was not locked and a brief look inside assured Gabe that it contained men's clothing, just as she said. He picked up a red silk house robe with peacocks and other multi-colored exotic birds. It smelled strongly of cologne and Gabe dropped it quickly. To each his own taste.

The larger portmanteau had some ledgers, probably removed from the bank. Interesting, but Gabe had neither the time now, nor the aptitude to read such ledgers. A deck of cards fingered by Gabe showed it was marked. It was what he expected. He was not surprised JR was cheating at cards. Too bad he could not read the bank ledgers. Regretfully, he closed the portmanteau and opened the second, smaller one.

"Good Gracious!" It was Priscilla who exclaimed, after she peaked inside with curiosity.

The portmanteau was filled with money. Bills tied together by a professional working at the bank. A lot of them.

"I had no idea," Priscilla said looking at Gabe

with widened eyes. "Are you going to take the money?"

"No, of course not. A man is entitled to carry as much cash as he has. I have no proof the money is not rightfully his. When I'll have it, however, I'll come after him."

CHAPTER 17

Pierce was having dinner together with Aunt Edith, in the kitchen at the large wooden table, as usual. The fact that Warner, his daughter, and occasionally his men preferred to dine formally in the dinning-room was a relief for Pierce. It was much more cozy and relaxed here in the kitchen, with Aunt Edith nearby.

To his surprise, Warner entered the kitchen and took a seat across the table from him. At least he left out his ever present smelly cigar, but there was going to be a confrontation. Pierce hated confrontations, especially at dinnertime. Captain, who was lying under the table at Pierce's feet, started to growl.

Warner looked at the dog with distaste. "Dogs are not allowed in this house," he said as an introduction, perhaps in order to assert his authority.

"They are now," Pierce said, continuing to look in his soup bowl.

Warner opened his mouth to object, then snapped it shut, thinking it was better to argue about what really mattered. A few days ago he wouldn't have hesitated to throw out the dog and force the boy to understand who was the master here and who gave the orders. Unfortunately, there was the sheriff to consider. Warner didn't want an open fight with him and until now the sheriff was willing to ignore the ranch. Why rile him up? And of course, Warner didn't want to admit it, but the way the boy handled himself in the knife fight with that idiot Stinky, showed he could not be dismissed easily.

"Luke told me that you fired the three cowboys taking care of the cattle. What were you thinking, boy? Where am I going to find men for that job, now in the middle of summer?"

Slowly, Pierce set down his spoon and thanked Aunt Edith for the tasteful soup. "Did Luke tell you also that they were changing the brand to cattle belonging to our neighbors?"

"Well, cattle wander from a ranch to another. It happens all the time. You didn't have to fire them for what the dumb animals were doing."

"They claimed they only obeyed your orders. Is it

true?" Pierce asked, nodding again his thanks to Aunt Edith who placed a plate full of roasting beef and potatoes in front of him.

"I told them to brand all the cattle on our land with Bar M. Yes. They did what they were supposed to do. I hope it's not too late to find them in town and call them back." Warner was drumming on the table with his fingers yellowed by long term tobacco use.

"It is too late. Even if I were so inclined to hire them back, which I'm not, they are currently in jail accused by John Gorman of stealing his cattle. There is also the matter of harboring a Wanted person, a train robber."

At this Warner raised his eyebrow in surprise. "I thought that idiot had already left."

"So you knew a train robber Wanted by the law was hiding on our land?"

Warner hit the table with his fist in anger. "You think life is as simple as that, boy? If you want to survive, you have to compromise. I didn't want my men killed and the house burned down because I refused to let a wounded man recover on this land. What he was, I don't know, I didn't ask. Where is he now?"

"At the doctor's, in town. His wound turned putrid. If he survives, he'll be taken in custody by the sheriff or by the marshals who were after him."

Warner bowed his head. "Maybe it's better this way. Now, about the men…"

"Don't worry, I already hired others to take care of the cattle," Pierce assured him.

"It's impossible. You can't find good men this time of year. How do you know they are reliable?"

"They were highly recommended," Pierce said not giving him more details.

"By who?"

"By our neighbor, John Gorman."

Warner exploded at this. He had a temper, but now the purple veins at his temple made Pierce afraid he'd be apoplectic. "Gorman hated me since he moved here last winter. Mark my words those men will rob us blind."

"I don't know about that. It was his missing cattle

being rebranded on our land, not the other way around." Pierce pushed away his empty plate and rose from his chair. "By the way, I want to see the ledgers. Have them ready for me tomorrow morning."

Warner frowned. "What ledgers?"

"The ranch books with all the expenses and income."

"They are on my desk somewhere."

"The ledgers on your desk have not been filled in two years. I assume you have the financial accounts kept up-to-date. I want to see them."

Warner coughed before answering. "What do you want to do with them? I bet you won't understand a thing."

"You would be wrong. After my parents died, a shrewd banker thought the same and threatened to foreclose on the farm for a bogus unpaid debt. I stayed up late many nights studying all sort of papers and even books about laws. In the end, I proved him wrong." As soon as he'd finished talking, Pierce knew it was a mistake and cursed his pride for boasting his knowledge.

It was better if the manager thought him a stupid farm boy. Now he might never see the real accounting.

He left the kitchen, while Warner cursed under his breath and Aunt Edith admonished him to put away the cigar or go outside to smoke.

Inside his room, Pierce lighted the gaslamp and heard Captain growling. He checked the room, looked in all corners, but found nothing. The dog, instead of quieting down, continued the low growl and the hair on the back of his neck bristled. Definitely a sign of danger. What could it be? Pierce saw nothing.

Then he saw a slight movement under the cover in bed. It was probably one of those silly pranks one does as a child. He grabbed the dog's collar trying to restrain him not to jump at the animal in bed.

"It's probably a skunk and we have to be careful. If he sprays us, we're doomed. Not even a year of washing daily is going to make the stench go away."

But it was not a skunk. When he pulled the cover away, slowly, a familiar rattle told him that whoever placed the snake in his bed had more than a childish prank in mind. The snake was coiled and ready to strike, so Pierce had no choice. He pulled out his gun and shot him twice in the head. His aim was quite accurate especially from such a small distance.

He looked at the dog, which was calmer and had ceased growling. Only then did he grab the bedsheets with the snake carcass and threw them out the window.

When he heard a soft knock on the door, Pierce thought it was Aunt Edith alerted by the gunshots. To his surprise it was not her. In the doorway, Vanessa was looking at him with her beautiful blue eyes. She was dressed in a long lacy nightgown over which she had an equally embroidered wrapper. Her unbound hair was all golden ringlets hanging down her back.

She stepped in and closed the door behind her. Should Pierce remind her of the proprieties? Maybe not. She knew better that it was not right for a maiden like her to be in his room alone with him. Pierce was sure she didn't give a fig about proprieties.

"I heard shots and didn't know what happened," she said as a way of explaining her presence there.

"As you see nothing happened," Pierce answered pointing at the bed. "I was making my bed."

"But the gunshots…"

"I like shooting flies off the wall."

She walked around the room, but there were not many personal belongings Pierce left out, so she came back to him. "Pierce, ever since we talked on the porch I thought about us."

"There is no us, Miss Vanessa," he pointed out gently. It was the truth. They lived in the same house, and yet they were in different worlds.

She touched his arm and leaned into him. "Oh yes, there is something special between us. Pierce. Life is short." Her hand glided up his arm. "I like a strong man and you proved to be the best. I know you want me, don't you?" she said raising her head and offering him her lips.

It was so tempting and he was only a simple man. "How could I not want you? You are the very picture of Beauty. Any man would be happy to call you his own."

"So what are you waiting for?" she asked a touch

of irritation in her voice, no doubt annoyed at his hesitation.

Pierce set her gently at a distance trying to break the spell she was weaving around him and to clear his mind. "It won't work, don't you see? You are here only temporarily. Not because your father will have to leave, but because this is not what you want in life. For you, living here is only a temporary necessity until you can find a better place. For me, this is my world. I feel a connection with this land and all I want is to take care of it until the day I die."

"But why?" she asked genuinely baffled. "It's not your land. It's your brother's. And even he doesn't want it."

"True. But I want it and I have an understanding with him. I'm not leaving. Not ever. Unlike my brother, I want this ranch to work and to see it prosper."

"You're a true farm boy," she said, only half derisive.

"Yes, at heart, I'm a man of the land. This particular land."

"All right. I understand that and I admit I've never liked living here so far from all civilization has to offer. I hate the dust and the smelly animals." She thought about it and then looked at him. "This doesn't explain why you reject me. Not many men would. You said you want me."

He smiled at her. "Rest assured Miss Vanessa that indeed not many men could resist your beauty and charm."

"You did."

"I had to. I've lost almost everything. My family, my brothers are scattered in all corners of the country. I gave up the farm in Kansas."

"Why, if you like farming as much as you do?"

"After my family died, I felt that part of my life ended. I had to start anew elsewhere. And I have to be careful when I choose my bride. She has to be hard working and willing to make a life here with me. It's not going to be easy. She will be my helpmate."

She pouted. "You're not going to find another beautiful woman like me."

"Certainly not. But beauty is not what I want most in a woman." He led her to the door. "Miss Vanessa, I know you don't need my advice, but don't sell yourself short. Chose a man who can give you everything that is important to you. Either love, or life in a big city with a lot of excitement, or material things, whatever you want. Don't run away with the first man who offers you a way out and don't marry a man because your father's interests are pushing you into that marriage."

The door opened suddenly and Warner stepped in. "What is going on here?"

"Cool down, Papa. He doesn't want me," Vanessa said.

Warner shook his finger at Pierce. "Have you been toying with my daughter's affection, young man?"

"No, sir. Your daughter's affection was not engaged in the least," Pierce answered tired of the whole drama.

"Papa," Vanessa stopped another righteous tirade from her father. "Pierce and I decided we don't suit after all. And just so you know, I've had it with this place. I'm leaving tomorrow to Chicago to Aunt Winnie. And no, I'm not going to marry that old goat you're pushing at me. Just so you know." With her head held high, regally, Vanessa left the room.

CHAPTER 18

He must have been out of his mind, Gabe thought walking back to the Sheriff's Office, absently looking at details that another time would have had his utmost attention, like a new stack of barrels near the mercantile or a glint in the sunlight on the roof of Kuster Hotel.

A moment of temporary insanity, that was it. Otherwise, there was no explanation what had possessed him to kiss the hatmaker. They were coming out of the closet and the space was awfully narrow, but that was no excuse for what happened. She turned to tell him to step around some boxes with ribbons stacked on the floor and she froze there looking at him. Her cornflower blue eyes were sparkling like sapphires in the semi-darkness and her chestnut hair was rich and lustrous.

With a will of its own, Gabe's hand reached to cup her face, marveling at the soft, velvety texture of her skin against his rough hand. If she would have stepped back or slapped his hand away, that would have been the end of it. No harm done. A coarse deputy sheriff who touched her cheek. Pardon me, ma'am. That's all.

But she didn't. On the contrary, she leaned into his palm and made a mewling sound, like a kitten asking to be petted. And here his brains got scrambled. Instead of getting out of there as fast as he could, he hugged her closer in his arms and his lips touched hers. Once he felt the sweet taste of her mouth he was lost, this was understandable. What man could step away? Not him, that's for sure.

He pulled her to him and indulged in the wonder of the moment. How long they kissed, he couldn't say. They'd been lucky that the entrance bell pealed in their foggy minds waking them to reality and the shrill voice calling, "U-hoo, Miss Priscilla, are you there?" had the effect of a bucket of iced water cooling their ardor.

The milliner patted her dress, then her hair, taming it in order. Then plastering the same professional smile on her face, she went to welcome her customer. "I was working in the back, Mrs. Kaufman. Good news, your lovely bonnet is ready."

What could Gabe do? He had to wait patiently

inside the narrow closet until Mrs. Kaufman tried on her new bonnet and some required adjustments were made and finally the matron, married to the owner of the lumber yard, left the store.

Only then was he free to mumble his excuses embarrassed and to leave the store, after looking furtively left and right into the street. He was no better than the banker's nephew, he thought disgusted. If he was in need of female company – and he had to admit that it had been quite a while – he should talk to one of the nice girls at the saloon. It was undignified for him to impose his attentions on the owner of the millinery. Not that she protested as she should. Yes, why didn't she, especially if she was carrying that scoundrel's baby?

His self-berating was interrupted when he reached the office and saw that Jeremiah was not at the desk. Live him to guard three moderately dangerous men and he got in trouble.

"I told you I don't have the keys," Jeremiah cried from the back room of the office where the jail was.

"You're lying," a rough voice told him. "Get us

out of here or I'll kill you like the rat you are."

"I will let you go, I promise."

It was time for Gabe to intervene. "You'll do no such thing Jeremiah or you'll be in trouble with the whole town, not only me." He stepped through the doorway in the space between the two cells. "What's going on here?"

What he saw was self-explanatory. One of the jailed men held Jeremiah by his coat and in his other hand he had a knife at his throat.

"Tsk, tsk. Where did he get the knife?" Gabe asked.

"I gave it to him to eat his meal," Jeremiah explained, crossing his eyes to see the knife threatening to cut him.

"Right," Gabe sighed exasperated. "That's what you usually see, the sheriff supplying the jailed men with knives." It was useless to try and reason with Jeremiah, hoping he'd be smarter than he was. Gabe drew his gun from his holster unhurriedly and twirling it around his finger expertly, he said, "You release him real easy now."

"Are you crazy? I have a knife at his throat. I'll kill him," the jailed man threatened.

Jeremiah whimpered when Gabe nodded. "Probably. Or maybe not. They say the good Lord protects the ones that are not too smart. On the other hand, I can assure you that I rarely miss and you'll be dead. Take your choices."

The man looked in Gabe's eyes and saw that behind the pleasant, even joking demeanor, there was a will of steel and a man who didn't hesitate to use his gun. He pushed Jeremiah away from the separating rails.

"I'll also take the knife to avoid the temptation," Gabe told him while placing his gun back in the holster.

The man threw the knife on the floor outside the jail cell.

"Jeremiah, pick it up and come with me." Gabe said and left the jail space.

He poured himself some coffee from the tin pitcher and sat in the chair behind the desk, prepared to tell Jeremiah a few choice words about what he should or should not do while in charge at the office. Not that Jeremiah would understand even if he wanted to get it right.

He didn't get to talk because the door opened and Dr. Pendergast came in. Assured that the doctor was not alarmed or in a state of panic and there was no emergency situation that required his presence, Gabe invited him to take a seat in front of him. "Coffee?" he asked.

"No, thank you. I had plenty this morning." The doctor placed on Gabe's desk a package wrapped in plain brown paper and tied with twine. He looked at Jeremiah, then at Gabe. "I'd like to talk to you in private."

It was not an unusual request. Gabe turned to Jeremiah. "Go and preach to the jailed men that what they did was wrong." Jeremiah's eyes filled with tears and mutely he shook his head. "Very well, then go outside and watch the street for any potential danger." This time his helper nodded eagerly and left the office. Gabe turned to the doctor. "Tell me what happened? I assume you came to tell me the wounded man didn't make it."

"You are correct. He's dead," the doctor confirmed.

Gabe scratched his stubble. He needed to shave. "The undertaker wants more money to bury him," he guessed.

"No. The sheriff doesn't need to pay for every man who dies in town. And in this case, the man had plenty of money on him to assure a decent burial." The doctor pointed to the package. "These are the rest of his belongings. A watch, a picture, and some money. What do you want to do with them?"

"His brother is right here, in jail. I'll give them to him."

"Oh, all right then." Pendergast made no move to leave. He fidgeted on his chair, rubbed his bald head, twisted the hat he'd placed on Gabe's desk, and finally said, "There is more. The man is dead, but not of his wounds. He's been shot in the head."

Gabe sat back in his chair surprised. "How?"

"I don't know. I found the office broken into this

morning. No money or medicine was taken, but the man was shot dead. It must have happened during the night. It was someone who knew what he was doing, because we live upstairs and heard nothing. My wife especially is a very light sleeper and nothing woke her up yesterday night."

"You know what is strange? The wounded man might have died of the infection anyhow. There was no need to shoot him. The killer must have been desperate to see him dead and not up and about, talking," Gabe mused in a loud voice.

"Yeah, probably," the doctor agreed. "Now I have to return to my office."

After the doctor left, Gabe went to the jail and opening the door, pointed his finger at the younger cowboy. "You, come on out."

"Why is he freed and not us?" the older one wanted to know.

Gabe locked the jail again without bothering to answer. He pushed the younger man to the front office room and closed the separating door. He sat at the desk and signaled the cowboy to take a seat in front of him.

"What's your name?"

"Jesse. Jesse Hardin."

He was not a bad young man. How had he ended up in this situation? Poverty? His brother's bad influcnce? "Your brother…," Gabe started to speak, wondering if there was a gentle way to say that his brother was dead.

"He died," the young cowboy anticipated, jumping up from the chair. "I want to see him. Please."

Seeing him was not a good idea, especially if he'd been shot in the head. "Jesse, please sit down. We need to talk." He pushed the package left by the doctor toward the young man. "These are his belongings and rest assured there was enough money that your brother will have a decent burial."

"I need to be there," he said.

Gabe agreed. "I'll take you there this afternoon when the undertaker sends word. But… you need to know that your brother didn't die of his wounds. He was shot in the head sometime during the night by a person who broke inside the doctor's office. I need you to tell me what enemies or friends your brother had and who could have done this."

"He was shot? But he was almost dying." The young man looked stunned.

"That's right. It could have been done for revenge, but I doubt it. It looks like the work of a person desperate to shut your brother up forever. I might be wrong, of course."

"I don't know much. There are the men who robbed the train, but those are dead or in prison." He hesitated. "There are no friends once a man takes this path in life. Only temporary partners and you have to be careful, they may kill you anytime to take your share. Or so Sam said. I know he met a man a few years ago when they both worked in the mine. It was hard work and it didn't pay well. I think he pushed Sam into robbing trains and banks, although the man is not actively taking part. He only plans the whole business. He is smart and very good with a gun. Sam admired him greatly. They were friends of sorts. Nah, I don't think he could have killed Sam. He knew Sam would never betray him."

"Do you know his name?"

The young man blinked, to chase away the tears from the corner of his eyes, then shook his head. "No. Sam talked about him, but he had a common name. John, Joe, Jack or something like that."

CHAPTER 19

The house was in uproar. Vanessa was going away just as she had promised she'd do and Warner was moving around her room, wringing his hands in disbelief.

"If you wait only a little time, I told you my business here can be concluded soon."

Vanessa shook her head, and closed the lid of her trunk with a final thudding sound. "No, Papa. I'm done waiting. I can't believe I've wasted my beauty and youth here. Three years in this dusty place, smelling of cow manure, isolated from the real world." She closed her smaller portmanteau and grabbed the hat box, looking around regretfully at the pretty hats and clothes she had to leave behind. "You'll have to send me the rest of my things at Aunt Hortense in Chicago. Now please go ask Luke to load my trunk in the buggy."

"You'll be back, girl. Mark my words. Because I'm through paying for your expensive fripperies. This is my reward. You leave me here in a lurch and run to your Aunt Hortense in Chicago," Warner said shaking his finger at her. Then he went to his office room and closed the door.

Vanessa shrugged. "Well, I suppose it was too much for you to understand that I'm suffocating here."

"Come on, it's not so bad." Smiling, Pierce leaned against the door jamb. "I'll drive you to the train station, princess." He grabbed the big trunk and hoisted it on his right shoulder, wincing at the pain he felt in the opposite one, where he'd been stabbed. Luckily his ribs felt better, almost healed.

His buggy had a large space behind the seat where he strapped the trunk with her portmanteau and hatbox on top.

Pierce patted his horse on the neck. "Be patient, Hero. I promise you a nice ride just the two of us every morning." The horse understood because he waited patiently to be harnessed to the buggy.

Warner didn't want to come out and the door to the office was closed.

"I said Good-bye to him," Vanessa muttered, waving at the two cowboys looking after their departing buggy.

It was a beautiful summer morning, not too hot yet, and for a while they drove in silence, which was unusual for the talkative Vanessa. "Look how nice the land is here. Don't you regret your decision to leave?" Pierce asked her.

She looked at him like he'd grown two heads. "Nice? I'll tell you what is nice. Busy streets in a big city, with elegant, polite people walking by, with window shops where one can see the newest creations in terms of fashion, the magnificent Marshall Field's store with several stories full of merchandise. Have you ever been to Chicago?"

"No, I haven't. I've been only once with Pa to Kansas City and I found it so crowded I wanted to get away fast. It's true. I'm a country boy at heart."

"Yes, well, to each his own. I wanted to tell you that in a way I'm grateful to you. What would I have done if you'd wanted to marry me and Pa thought that it would suit his interest?"

At this, Pierce laughed. "You'd have done what

you intended to do regardless of my wanting to marry you or not. You intended to string me along as your father told you to do, without ever being serious about marriage. Why don't you admit it?" he said patting her knee good-naturedly.

She frowned at him. "Probably. I'm not ready to marry yet. It's so much more fun to flirt and see all the men bawled over by me." She looked at him from under her long lashes. "I guess you think I'm a bad woman."

"No, Miss Vanessa, you are, the way you are. Beautiful without equal and a force to reckon with."

"But you wouldn't marry me," she tested him.

"No, I wouldn't," he agreed readily. "And you wouldn't marry me either. We have entirely different goals in life. We are different. We've had this conversation before and agreed we don't suit."

"Yes, we did. This is the reason why I want to thank you. You opened my eyes to following my own path and goals in life."

Pierce nodded. "Right. It would be a pity to marry an old man even if he were rich and could give you everything you desired."

She giggled like a little girl caught doing mischief. "Better to marry a young rich man. That's what I intend to do in Chicago. My aunt moves in high society circles. I intend to take my time, enjoy life in town, shopping, parties, and search for the right one without any haste." She clapped her hands in joy. "Yes, that's what I'll do."

She was quite a feisty woman Miss Vanessa, Pierce thought. Not as bad or haughty as people thought. Out of her pampered comfortable world in the city, she reacted with disdain at this rougher world. Her father didn't understand her at all. Or maybe he did, but tried to use her for his own interest.

They reached town and were driving toward to train depot, when Pierce saw ahead of them a slim, young boy, with a cap pulled low on his head, trudging along the way. He stopped the buggy.

"I'll be back in a moment, Miss Vanessa," he assured her and jumped down, running to talk to the boy. "Pst, Amy, It's me Pierce."

"I know. I saw you driving with her Highness."
She looked at him askance and moved on.

He stopped her. "Amy, wait. It's not what you
think. Vanessa is going away. I'm taking her to the train
station. After that, I'll come talk to you. Are you going to
the milliner's shop?"

She nodded. "Yes. That's what I do in the
morning."

He raised his hand to touch her face, then thought
better of it. "Are you all right?"

She shrugged. "Yeah. As usual."

"Listen, Amy. I have to go, but I'll be back to talk
to you in about an hour, after the train leaves. It's
important." Reluctant, he turned to go back to the waiting
buggy. Amy didn't say more. She continued to walk to
the store without looking up when the buggy passed by
her.

"Sorry," he said to Vanessa. "I had to talk to a
friend."

"Mmm, You made me curious, Pierce. What's
her story?"

"There's no story. He's poor boy, cleaning at the saloon," he explained vaguely.

"I'm many things, but stupid is not one of them. That was a woman dressed as a young boy," Vanessa looked at him sharply. "Why is she hiding?"

"Because what I told you was true. She's cleaning at the saloon. She's poor and has no one to stand up for her."

"No one but you."

"I had nothing to offer her. How could I protect her when my own situation was uncertain?"

Vanessa touched his hand. "Do what you have to do, Pierce, just don't kill my father."

He nodded. "I'll do my best to end this peacefully. Of course, if he personally draws his gun on me, I'll have to do the same."

"Yes, I know. Usually, he likes to plan and plot and hire people to do the dirty job for him, so hopefully it won't come to a direct confrontation."

The buggy stopped in front of the train station and Pierce unloaded her luggage and carried it on the platform. There, she extended her hand to him.

"Good-bye, Pierce. I wish you luck to achieve what you want." Slowly, she rose on tiptoes and kissed his cheek. Then she smiled at him a little melancholy.

"All the best to you too, Miss Vanessa. But it's not yet time to say Good-bye. There's still another half hour until the train arrives."

"It is time. I don't like long Good-byes. Thank you for bringing me here. Go now."

"Are you sure?"

"Yes. I'll be perfectly safe waiting here for the train."

So, he left. He looked back one more time, but Vanessa had entered the depot's waiting room. Pierce climbed back in the buggy and drove to the milliner's store.

When he entered the store, he pulled his hat off, a bit intimidated by the utterly feminine character of the place. Just when he was ready to back away, a young woman came from the back smiling at him, ready to assist.

He knew Miss Priscilla and this was not she. "Ma'am, I'd like to…" he stopped and did a double take. "Amy? Is that you?"

She twirled smiling. "How do I look? Miss Priscilla decided that I should live with her, at least for now. This is an old dress of hers. Isn't it lovely?" she said smoothing imaginary creases from the silky fabric. "It's a moiré taffeta. Isn't it fabulous?" The fabric was a little faded and had been washed and ironed countless times, but Amy looked pleased and happy. Pierce almost decided to give up on what he'd wanted to talk to her about.

"So you're not going back working or living at the saloon," he wanted to know.

"No, I'm not. A few more months with a second paying job would have been helpful, but Miss Priscilla assured me that looking like that, I could have a better chance finding work at the hotel."

Pierce shuffled his feet and looked down, studying the pattern in the carpet. "Amy, you don't have to. I have a better idea. You could marry me," he blurted out.

Amy blinked. "Marry you? But we just met a few days ago. We don't know each other."

"So what? This is the west. Mail order brides were common until a few years ago. I know every woman wants to be courted. But I don't have time to come to town so often. I won't lie to you. I don't have much to offer. If I succeed to clean up the ranch of all the unsavory characters, my brother promised me half the ranch. It's good land and he does not want to live there. We could make a good life there." He stopped embarrassed. At home, it seemed like a great idea and a solution for all of Amy's woes. Now he was not so sure.

"I don't know what to say, Pierce. I've always dreamed of marrying for love, not for material reasons," she answered hesitantly.

"In time, perhaps you could love me. I will always treat you with respect and I take my marriage vows seriously."

"Do you love me?" she asked.

"As you said, we don't know each other well, but

you are all I want in a wife."

"I'm not beautiful like Vanessa."

He sighed wondering how to explain that she was indeed his choice bride. How could he convince her that he didn't ask on a whim, but that he had thought very well about this? "Vanessa is not as bad as people imagine. She belongs to a different world and would never settle here or be happy with life on a ranch. It's all a matter of character. You grew up in a big city, but you are adaptable. I feel that you'll make our house a home and be happy wherever that would be. Am I wrong?"

CHAPTER 20

Pierce left Amy befuddled and confused and he wondered if he'd bungled the proposal so badly that she'd not even consider it. It was a pity because he realized that Amy was perfect for him. She was hard-working, honest, and determined to fight to survive no matter how difficult life was. Like him, Amy had close to nothing and no one to help her, but this didn't faze her or make her less certain of her desire to succeed. His Amy was a feisty one. They could make a good life together.

As for love, Pierce could respect her and be true to her. He didn't know what else was expected of him. Certainly not what his father had shown his mother all their life, a sour face and disparaging words of disapproval, no matter how hard his mother worked to make a home for their family. Love was not the fearful looks his mother had any time his father entered the house and her permanent attempt to shield the children from his upset mood and frightening anger.

Pierce figured that if he avoided all this and made

sure that in his house there were smiles and laughter and praise all the time, he'd prove his love better than his father.

Before passing, his mother had slipped off her finger the old ring that had belonged to his grandmother and she had given it to him. It was a thin gold band with three small garnets. Before leaving Amy, despite what she said that she needed time to think, he placed the ring on her finger. She protested, but didn't remove it and didn't give it back to him. He understood why when she looked at it in awe and whispered, "Nobody ever gave me a gift like that." So, there was hope for him yet.

Pierce drove his buggy along the road to the ranch and was lost in thought. Absently, he observed a cloud of dust in front of him. Two riders were approaching at high speed. They stopped at a short distance in front of him and he recognized the two remaining men hired by Warner, Luke and the other one.

"Look at that, it's the farmer boy," Luke said, leaning forward over the pommel.

The other one looked at Luke for a clue, then

draw out his gun. "It was a mistake to come back, boy. Haven't you learned anything from your… accidents?" he laughed exposing his yellow teeth with a missing one in front.

Taking his time, he raised his arm, aimed in the general direction of the buggy, and fired a shot. He missed by a mile. This shot was intended only to scare Pierce. It upset his horse. Hero rose on his hind legs pawing the air with his front ones, very nervous.

The next shots came in rapid succession after the first and much closer to the target than the first. There was no use staying up in the buggy seat like a sitting duck. Pierce jumped down and drawing his own gun fired in the general direction of the gunfighter. His aim was better and the man slumped in the saddle, over the pommel, face down. The gun slipped from his hand and fell to the ground discharging close to his friend's horse.

Luke, who until that moment had only watched the bullet exchange from the same position atop his horse, looked at his companion in disbelief. First, he pulled the reins tight, to control his agitated horse. Then he drew his own gun and fired at Pierce, who was trying to get up from where he was laying on the ground. It was a clear shot, aimed to kill.

It didn't kill Pierce only because he moved to the side and the bullet caught him in the shoulder. It was his left shoulder, the one where he had his knife wound that was not entirely healed. The pain was so sharp that Pierce dropped his gun and grabbed his shoulder with his right hand, falling back on the ground.

He was in agony.

Luke dismounted and came near him. "Well, farmer boy, that was a lesson for you. Warner told us to toy with you and chase you away. Not to kill you. I think he was wrong to fear the sheriff's retribution. You are a pest that is not going away. I'm going to get rid of you forever. Who's to know it? They'll find your dead body here and no one will know who shot you. I'm betting no one will care."

It was possibly true that no one would care, but he was not dead yet. Pierce looked up. Luke was standing near him and a gunshot would hit Pierce straight where Luke was aiming. Certain of his advantage, Luke was talking and boasting, probably wanting to see Pierce grovel with fear.

Pierce looked to where his gun had fallen nearby, but Luke saw it too, and he fired making the gun move farther away. Pierce calculated his chances and he saw no other way to get the gun. He clenched his teeth and braced himself against the pain. With both hands, he grabbed the boot near him and pulled hard on the man's foot.

Luke lost his balance and fell backwards. He didn't release his gun. However, the few seconds were enough for Pierce to roll away trying to get his own gun.

It was too far away. In a fraction of a second, he saw Luke sit up and raise his gun. Pierce read the determination to kill in his eyes. A shot rang out and Luke's eyes mirrored surprise before falling back on the ground, the gun slipping from his hand.

Pierce looked behind him and saw a stranger atop of a black stallion. He had an olive complexion, dark hair and eyes. He looked fierce and his Winchester was still smoking from the shot. "I don't like uneven odds. And I don't like Luke Clanton. He was ready to kill you, if I had not shot him first."

"I am mighty grateful to you. May I know who saved my life?" Pierce asked, getting up and picking up his gun.

"I'm Maitland. Elliott Maitland. I'm a rancher farther down the road. And who might you be, son? I haven't seen you around here. The only man with a buggy is the good Dr. Pendergast, when he is called to one of the ranches."

"I'm Pierce Monroe."

"Ah, the sheriff's younger brother. John Gorman told me about you. I thank you for returning our cattle to us."

Pierce grabbed the side of the buggy to steady himself. He felt lightheaded from the blood loss from his new wound. "Feel free to inspect the rest of the cattle on Bar M Ranch and take yours back. I fired the cowboys who changed the brand. But I had no time to go see how the cattle are faring."

THE YOUNGER BROTHER

Maitland dismounted. "Don't worry. You can rely on Tom Bald Eagle." He came closer and briefly examined Pierce's wound. He helped him climb up in the buggy. "You have to go to town to see the doctor. The bullet is still inside and it needs to come out. You're lucky I'm going there myself."

Maitland checked the gunfighter slumped in the saddle. "This one's dead," he concluded. When he did the same with Luke he shook his head in wonder. "What do you know? He's like the proverbial cat with nine lives. No one escapes alive from my Winchester, yet he's only wounded. He might live to plague other people." Saying this, Maitland hoisted Luke over his shoulder and he threw him across the saddle of Luke's horse without much care.

Then he tied the three horses, including his own stallion, at the back of the buggy. When Pierce tried to force his eyes to stay focused and wondered where he'd find the strength to drive back to town, Maitland climbed up in the seat near Pierce, took the reins, and made a clicking sound, signaling Hero to start moving. He turned the buggy around and drove to town.

"Me, in a buggy. I'll be the laughingstock of town," he muttered.

"Not so. It's very practical," Pierce answered before falling in a blessed stupor, where there was no sharp pain burning in his shoulder.

Gabe McCarthy needed answers. He decided to go visit the banker first. The clerk looked at him frightened and Gabe wondered why. He didn't say he wanted to arrest the banker. He said he wanted to talk. Soon he understood the source of the clerk's fear was not Gabe. A woman could be heard shouting even through the closed door of the banker's office.

The door opened and she exited in a huff. She was in her thirties and could have been considered pretty if not for the signs of too early dissipation that took a toll on her youth and prettiness.

"You'll be hearing from me. I don't need a lawyer to get what is rightfully mine," she said. Noticing Gabe for the first time, her demeanor changed on the spot and a rehearsed smile lit her over-powdered face. "I haven't seen you before. Are you new in town?"

"Somewhat," Gabe answered, while the clerk was wringing his hands.

"Well, I don't have time now, but this town sure looks more interesting," she said and with a last flutter of her eyelashes she left the bank.

"You can go in, Deputy," the clerk told Gabe, while going back to his place behind the counter.

Gabe entered closing the door behind him, although he shouldn't have worried. The other customers were too busy commenting on the drama that had unfolded in the office. The banker was standing in front of the window looking outside with his hands in his pockets. When he heard the door closing, he turned around and he invited Gabe to take a seat in front of his desk.

"Are you married, Deputy?"

"No, sir. Never been."

The banker nodded in approval. "Good. Neither was I until two years ago. And if you think, as most people do in this town, that I was attracted by a young pretty face, you'd be wrong. Approaching sixty, I felt the burden of my age and I got fooled by her lying words that she wanted a child as much as I did. That is what I wanted from her, an heir to carry my name and follow in my steps."

It was more than Gabe needed to know. As always when people started to unburden their secrets, he was embarrassed for them. "I don't know the lady."

The banker looked at him sharply. "You will. She's been away, trying her luck in Texas, but now that she's back, you'll hear about her. Wherever Cora Lynn is, trouble follows. Mark my words."

"Yes, Mr. Turner. We'll deal with that when it happens. Now I wanted to ask you a few details connected to your nephew."

"Ah, JR. Another burden I have to bear in life. I was hoping he'll either go away or straighten out and make an honest way in life. He did neither."

"My investigation into the death of a traveling card player led me to your nephew." He raised his hand to prevent the banker from drawing conclusions. "I'm not saying he's guilty. But he was close by when the gambler was shot. Entirely by accident, I discovered a bag with money belonging to your nephew. So my question is, how much money did he steal from the bank before you fired him?"

The banker bent his head, then wiped his perspiring brow. For a moment, Gabe thought he was not going to answer, but the banker surprised him with a straight look. "Seventeen thousand. Sheriff Monroe searched his room at the hotel and found nothing. Zilch. I had to reimburse the bank from my own money. The prestige of my business and the trust of our customers are of utmost importance to me. I returned every penny that was missing."

"I see. I'm sorry to insist, are you sure of this amount?" It was a staggering amount, enough for a family to live comfortably for a long time.

"Of course I am. I did the accounting twice and I know how much money I had to reimburse. Did you find it?"

It was a situation with legal implications and for the first time Gabe cursed the sheriff for chasing after outlaws and leaving him to solve this. "Yes, sir. Legally the money belongs to your nephew and I have to prove he is guilty of a crime in order to take it from him."

"That's all? I can give you proof that he stole from the bank."

It would be easier if the theft was proved. "You can?"

The banker raised his eyebrow haughtily. "I might be an old fool, who was taken by a woman's pretty face and by my nephew's reassuring words, but as a banker, I know what I'm doing. I can smell a cooked book and false accounting at once. I have plenty of proof. I haven't used it until now because if he didn't have the money either in a separate account in the bank or hidden in his room it was pointless to see him in jail. Now, if you say you found it, then I officially demand its return."

"The return of the seventeen thousand?"

"Yes. Didn't I say I can prove JR stole every penny of it?"

Gabe exhaled loudly before speaking. "All right. What about the rest?"

"What rest?"

"The remaining money. There were almost forty thousand in your nephew's portmanteau."

For the first time, the banker looked at him open-mouthed, speechless.

CHAPTER 21

Maitland brought Pierce to the doctor's office, then unloaded the unconscious, wounded Luke in the next room. After talking to Dr. Pendergast and making sure that Pierce was in good hands, he left to talk to the sheriff and to take the body of the second gunfighter to the undertaker for burial.

Dr. Pendergast washed his hands and assisted by a scary woman, tall and severe looking, he started to probe Pierce's wound. At first, he was brave and clenched his teeth against the searing hot pain, but after several of the doctor's attempts to find the bullet, he couldn't bear it any longer and cried out in pain. The nurse stuck a piece of leather between his teeth to bite on it. Lucky for him, shortly after that, the doctor extracted the bullet with a grunt of satisfaction and dropped it in a nearby tray.

By then, Pierce was ready to pass out. Whatever the doctor applied to clean his wound, camphor or turpentine, burned him and he closed his eyes certain that he was going to faint. He didn't, but after his shoulder was bandaged, he fell asleep blessedly welcoming the oblivion that came with it after his ordeal.

In the afternoon, he had a series of visitors. The first one was Gabe McCarthy. In fact, when he opened his eyes, Gabe was there, near his bed, slouched in a chair.

"Hey kid," he said when he saw that Pierce woke up. "I think you're in over your head."

"Hmm," Pierce answered. His shoulder was still burning, but the pain was less intense, almost bearable. "Where is Bill?" he asked.

"Up in the mountains, near Centennial. You'd better tell me what happened."

Pierce thought about all he'd been through since arriving at the ranch. "Gabe, I think I did it. I cleaned the ranch of all Warner's men. The three cowboys taking care of cattle were caught while changing brands and harboring a wounded outlaw, the train robber."

Gabe nodded. "The ones brought to the Sheriff's Office by Gorman's men."

Pierce face fell. "You mean that if Gorman helped me, Bill will not admit that I managed to do it alone." Disappointment rang clear in his voice.

"No, kid. Bill is an honest man. He'll keep his promise. Besides, there is nothing wrong with getting help from your neighbors. On the contrary, both John Gorman and Elliott Maitland are tough ranchers. It's remarkable that you gained their trust and they helped you. Now, about today, who shot you?"

"I drove Vanessa to the train station in the buggy," Pierce said and Gabe's eyebrows shot up in surprise, but he made no comment. "Then I went to the milliner's and asked Amy to marry me." He saw no point in keeping this a secret, not from Gabe whom he considered to be his friend, closer than his own brother Bill, who'd made it clear he had no need to get to know Pierce.

"Jeez! You were busy this morning," Gabe observed.

"When I was driving back to the ranch, the two remaining gunfighters hired by Warner attacked me. One of them started shooting at me. At first he just wanted to scare me, then he shot to kill. I fired back at him as you taught me and he was hit. Maitland said he was dead."

"And who shot you?"

"The other one, Luke. He wanted to kill me. I was lucky Maitland was there and saved my life. He shot Luke. You can see him in the other room."

"I already did. He was hit in the gut. Ugly looking wound. It's a miracle he's still alive. He's not going away anytime soon even if he survives."

Pierce was tired. "Anyhow, Warner is the only one left at the ranch and he is powerless without his men. He likes to order others to do his work."

"Hmm," Gabe cleared his voice. "Don't underestimate Warner, kid. I feel there is more to this story than a simple rustling operation. That's only part of it."

"You might be right," Pierce agreed, no matter how much he disliked the idea.

The doctor entered the room to check on Pierce. Gabe left promising to come back later on. The doctor looked at his wound and wrapped it again with clean gauze. Just then, a second visitor came in. It was Amy, dressed as a young lady this time and very agitated.

"Pierce, I heard that you were wounded badly," she said taking a seat in the chair near the bed.

"Nah, it's only a scratch," Pierce said looking at Dr. Pendergast who was washing his hands. He had this habit to wash before and after examining a patient. Pierce had never seen anyone, even a doctor, wash so frequently. The doctor shook his head, but didn't contradict him.

Amy looked after the doctor as he left the room. When the door was closed, she took Pierce's hand. "I thought a lot about what you told me. I'm sorry, Pierce, I don't think it is a good idea for us to marry. It will be a foolish thing to do in haste that we'll regret later on." Sniffing, she took off the ring he gave her, looked at it one more time with regret, and placed it in his hand.

Pierce was stunned. He closed his fist over the ring. "Why?" he asked. A lot of possibilities crossed his mind. Perhaps his grandma's ring was too small, but

Amy was a poor person of modest means. She didn't expect rich jewelry, not when they had to make the ranch work first. In fact, this was one of the reasons Pierce was attracted to her. Because she was like him, with the same ideals in life. Had he been wrong?

She fidgeted in the seat. "Because we don't know each other well and you lead a dangerous life. Look at you. Someone used you for target practice and shot you."

"Dangerous life? This from the girl who dressed as a boy and lived in danger in a saloon. Really?"

"Well, that was different," she said gathering her skirts to stand up and go.

Pierce grabbed her hand. "The truth, Amy. You owe me the truth."

She collapsed back in the chair. "The truth is I panicked. I'm on the verge of building a life on my own, without being at a man's whim and I'm afraid to change it. Miss Priscilla asked me if I knew you well and I realized I know next to nothing about you. I meant to ask you to wait, but I know you are busy at the ranch and it wouldn't be fair to ask this of you." She smiled at him sadly. "I guess I am not meant to be a mail order bride."

"No, you are not. You've made a life for yourself without needing a man to support you. I'm proud of you and it is one of the reasons I thought we'll get along well." He moved his arm and winced when the pain shot through his shoulder. "I don't know, maybe I look young, but I'm twenty-six years old and I know well what I want in life. Don't you want to give me… us a chance?"

She bit her lower lip hesitating, but then thought better of it and shook her head. "I'm sorry, Pierce." And she was gone.

"Well son, women are strange creatures, difficult to understand," the doctor said coming back into the room. Pierce wondered if he'd been listening behind the door. "My own wife demanded a lot of courting and running around before she consented to marry me and follow me wherever there was need for my services."

Pierce thought of the tall, unpleasant woman and it seemed unlikely that the short, good-natured doctor had to work so hard to get her to say yes to his proposal.

THE YOUNGER BROTHER

The third visitor came when darkness had enveloped the town and Pierce had been lulled to sleep by the loud snoring he heard upstairs.

He was dreaming of a ball where he and Amy were waltzing together. A persistent noise woke him up. It was a warm night and the window was open to allow the breeze to cool the room.

Pierce opened his eyes just in time to see a dark silhouette pushing the window open wider. The stranger climbed over the window sill and landed inside the room. Pierce checked the nightstand, but his gun was not there. He could see well in the dark and it was clear that the intruder had a gun in his hand. What could he do? He pretended to be asleep.

In three steps, the stranger was near the bed. He grabbed Pierce's collar and shook him. "No more tricks. Tell me where it is. Where did you hide it?"

The shaking jarred his wounded shoulder and his resolution to be quiet and play dead vanished. Pierce emitted a loud howl of pain.

That made the stranger let go of his shirt.

"I don't know what you're talking about," Pierce protested.

"Who are you?" the stranger asked.

"Excuse me, you break into my room and then you ask me to introduce myself?" Pierce objected.

Not a good idea. The stranger grabbed his shirt again. "Don't pretend you don't know. If you're in cahoots with Luke Colton, then you should know. I'm asking again, where is the money?"

Another shaking followed and Pierce couldn't bear it. The gun was not on the nightstand, but there was a large pitcher with water. He grabbed it with his good hand and tried to hit the other man to make him let go of his shirt. He didn't do too much damage, but the cold water had an unpleasant effect on his attacker who let go of him.

His survival instinct kicked in and he rolled out of bed and on the floor in the exact moment that the stranger's gun discharged where he'd been a second before.

Pierce was aware that a bullet would find him

soon, unless he could get a better weapon himself.

Lucky for him, the door opened and the doctor came in, carrying a lantern in his hand. "What is going on here?"

The intruder turned to him, but decided killing the doctor was not a good idea. He jumped over the window sill and vanished into the night.

"Maybe we shouldn't take care of all this riffraff that brings dubious characters after them with intent to kill, Alfred," the wife said coming in after the doctor.

Pierce was ready to protest at being called riffraff, when the doctor said, "That is not a Christian thought, my dear. My oath requires that I take care of all people, honest or not, rich or poor alike."

His wife raised her chin and left the room huffing.

"That's a noble thought, Doctor," Pierce said looking in dismay at the bed sheet that had a bullet hole in it.

The doctor quickly picked up the broken pitcher and changed the sheet with a freshly washed one. "Go to bed, son."

CHAPTER 22

Gabe McCarthy was in a bad mood. There was a killer roaming through town and he needed to find him fast. Angel, the girl from the saloon had almost told him who he was, but was frightened into silence by a gun fired from outside her window.

Of course, it was possible that the death of the gambler in a back alley was not connected to the killing of the wounded train robber in the doctor's office. The young man who called Gabe out could have been just a silly young man bragging about his prowess with a gun. And perhaps JR Turner was only an ambitious nephew who wanted to take over his uncle's business. Yes, maybe they were not connected at all, but instinct told Gabe that they were. It made Gabe crazy that he was not able to discover the real culprit and to understand who was pulling the strings.

He was doing his nightly rounds and tonight he was determined to pay close attention to all the unusual movements and details that might make the killer reveal himself.

The saloon was lighted and the music was loud. The new piano player was better than the old one who used to repeat only three songs, again and again. At first glance, everything was as it should be. The same drunk cowboys standing at the bar, the gamblers at the tables, the girls mingling among them, pouring more drinks and laughing out loud. There were some new faces too; that was unavoidable since the transcontinental railroad passed through town and brought newcomers every day.

A man, slightly unsteady on his feet, approached the piano player and requested a repeat of the previous tune. He threw a coin on the floor near the player, who nodded and started the song over again.

Nothing unusual, Gabe concluded. His attention migrated to the two tables with active card players. Two new figures in town. One looked like a traveling salesman, jovial and complaining loudly about his bad luck. He was mostly looking for company, wanting to avoid spending the night alone in his hotel room. The second man was not so easy to place in a category. He was mostly quiet, minding his cards, with his hat covering half his face. He was losing and winning equally and he was not drinking. Also he wore thin leather gloves. That detail was not uncommon for gunfighters, even if it was the middle of summer. Some preferred to wear gloves, to draw faster and unimpeded in case their hands were dirty or slippery.

Gabe went to the bar. "All is well, Tom?" he asked the owner of the saloon, who acted as barman tonight.

"I can't complain, Deputy. Business is good, customers are plenty and if they don't break my mirror…" He looked over his shoulder at the large mirror covering half the wall behind the bar. "…and if they don't shoot my Danae…" He pointed up at the voluptuous naked lady in the painting above the mirror. "…then all is well," he concluded. Tom Wilkes continued wiping the glasses, knowing better than to offer Gabe a drink while he made his nightly rounds.

Gabe made his way near Angel who was trying half-heartedly to charm a cowboy and to entice him to buy her a drink. Unfortunately for her, he was too far gone into his own drink to react. Angel shrugged and leaned her elbows on the bar counter.

"Angel," Gabe whispered. He had his back to the counter facing the room. "I hope you've changed your mind about giving me the information I want. Who was in the saloon the night the gambler was killed? Who was at his table? Is JR Turner the one you're afraid of?" He turned his head and looked at her.

She hesitated, torn between the desire to confide in him and the fear of placing her own life in danger. A body came between them. The man at the gaming table. "Well girl, aren't you supposed to entertain all the customers instead of propping the bar here?" he asked in a rough, hoarse voice. He dropped two coins on the counter despite not drinking anything. The coins prevented Tom Wilkes to answer in kind, not that he would defend one of the girls by contradicting a customer.

The words made Angel look down meekly, and Gabe didn't see the terror in her eyes, as he, himself looked fascinated at the stranger's left hand, ungloved this time, pushing his coins over the counter. A puckered scar, shaped like a half moon was imprinted in the flesh.

Angel walked away quickly. By the time Gabe remembered why the scar was so familiar although he'd never seen it before, the stranger had turned around and left the saloon.

Gabe sprinted after him. Outside the saloon, he paused getting used to the darkness after the bright light inside. Cautiously, he looked around for signs of a live presence. Footsteps running away on 1st Street toward the train depot propelled Gabe in that direction. At the corner with Ivinson Street he looked toward Kuster Hotel only a block away and saw an open window upstairs with the curtain fluttering in the breeze. Except that there was no breeze right then. Someone was moving inside the room, looking outside through the sheer curtain.

He looked back toward the train depot. The chance of finding someone by checking the many buildings of the depot and the warehouses was slim. Also he could be ambushed easily, so Gabe turned left on

Ivinson Street to the hotel.

At that late hour, only the old janitor was in the lobby carrying a broom and a half empty pail. Gabe entered, avoiding the wet spots on the floor and trying not to leave dirty traces on the freshly washed wood boards.

"Hello, Paddy. Where is the front desk man?" Gabe asked the janitor smiling.

The janitor propped himself on the broomstick. "He stepped out for a moment. There isn't too much need of him at this hour. Do you have business with him, Deputy?" The old man was dressed in worn clothes, fit for his work, and in general, his humble posture caused him to be ignored by guests of the hotel and locals as well. Nobody paid any attention to him. Very few people knew that old Paddy was aware of most comings and goings in the hotel.

"No. You are the one I want to talk to. Have you seen any unusual persons entering the hotel?"

"Not since Lily Rosetti, that Italian singer. I can't say I've seen someone more unusual," the old janitor answered.

Gabe shook his head smiling. "I wasn't asking about that sort of unusual person. How about the banker's nephew, JR Turner? What is his room?"

"I wouldn't know about him," the janitor answered shrewdly. "He's always complaining of not having warm water in his room early in the morning. Jenny is running ragged, first to do his bidding, him being a guest of the hotel, and then to escape his roving hands. Once I walked past Room 107 and I saw him in a heated talk with another man, dressed all in black like them gunslingers."

Gabe's attention perked up. "When was that?"

The janitor scratched his head. "Oh, first about month ago, and then again, just yesterday. Jenny said that the other man had Turner by the collar and was shaking him like a puppet. He asked him 'Where is it?' about whatever he was looking for." Paddy, the janitor sniffed and asked, "Is Turner in trouble?"

Gabe understood that Turner's obnoxious behavior didn't endear him much to the hotel personnel who would have liked to see him taken down a peg. "He could be," he admitted. "I have to talk to him and ask him a few questions."

"Too bad you don't know his room number. Maybe the night clerk will tell you when he comes back, although we are not allowed to give information about our guests." He winked at Gabe and taking his pail and broom, he walked to the back of the lobby, behind the staircase.

Gabe climbed the stairs quickly and walked on the carpeted hallway looking for room 107. Once in front of the door he placed his ear close to the door, but didn't hear any noise or conversation inside. He knocked on the door, but no one answered. He knocked again briefly and tried the handle. The door opened easily. He hesitated to enter, stepping to one side to peer in the room through the crack of the door. This saved his life because someone in the dark room shot at him.

Drawing his gun, Gabe jumped inside and dropped instantly to the floor, rolling closer to the wall. The other person fired again and this time Gabe heard him muttering and cursing. "You're not going to get me, you hear? I'll kill you."

Gabe rolled his eyes. He placed his gun back in his holster. "Turner, hold your fire. It's Deputy Sheriff McCarthy here."

A deep breath of relief was followed by a dull thud of an object hitting the floor. Hoping that was Turner's gun, Gabe stood up slowly and lighted the gas lamp in the corner. When there was finally light in the room, Gabe turned to search for the banker's nephew. He found him sitting prostrate on the floor, between the bed and the window, moving rhythmically back and forth.

"He tried to kill me, do you know that?" Turner wailed.

Possible, but somewhat doubtful, Gabe thought. If there was money involved, then the mystery man needed to know where Turner had hidden it. Killing him was not going to achieve that. Most probably the man wanted to scare him into giving him the money or telling him where it was. Did Turner break and tell the man about the closet at the milliner's? "Tell me his name and where I can find him and I'll get it for you."

Turner pshawed. "His name… is Joe Smith." He nodded. "That is the name he used recently. Nobody knows his real name. I wonder if even he remembers it. As for where he lives, don't expect a nice house with picket fence and a sweetheart at the window waiting for him. Not even a hotel room or boardinghouse. Who knows in what outlaws' hole he is spending his time plotting nefarious things?"

Taking a seat in a chair near the table with a good view of both the window and the door, Gabe focused on Turner's last words. "What nefarious things?" he asked.

Finally more relaxed with a deputy in the room, Turner stood up and grabbing a whiskey bottle from the nightstand, poured a shot in the glass near it and gulped it down without inviting Gabe to join him, not that Gabe was in the mood for a drink. "I have not the least idea," he said shrugging. "I'm a banker, not an outlaw. He could have done whatever – rob stores or banks, attack trains, you name it." He saw Gabe's doubtful look and he set his glass down, turning to him. "I don't care if you believe me or not. It's not in my character to fraternize with people like him or to soil my hands doing these kinds of things."

Well, for someone who didn't shy away from stealing from his uncle's bank or gambling every night at the saloon, it was strange to claim such high principles. The only reason Gabe was inclined to believe him was because young Turner was a lazy man. He probably considered attacking trains or robbing stores too much work and risk and plainly not worth it when there were other ways to siphon money from his uncle's bank into his own pocket.

"How did you get involved with him?" Gabe asked.

Turner pondered if there was any risk in telling a lawman, but if Gabe could get rid of Smith, it was worth it. "He came to me when I was in charge of the bank and asked me to keep his money safe. Not in a regular account, but in a safe place where he could find it when he needed. In exchange, I was to have a generous percentage of it. I had no idea of its provenance. It could have been from robbing trains and other similar sources, but as a banker, I don't have to ask my customers where they got their money."

"Ah, I wondered…," Gabe said in a low voice. "So did you accept it?"

"Of course, I'd have been crazy not to accept such a deposit."

Gabe sighed. "Right. So, how come you had a fall out?"

Turner sat on the edge of the bed. "The crazy man wants the money now. It would have been easier if I were still in charge at the bank, but now it's more difficult to access it and remove it… I'll do it of course, but my hands are tied and I need more time to do it safely. After all, we're talking about a lot of money, not a hundred or two. You understand, don't you?"

Oh yes, Gabe understood well. Especially now, after being fired from the bank, young Turner decided that he could keep all the money. After all, there was no official account or receipt for the money. Only a verbal deal and understanding. If the money was ill gotten gains, there was no way that Smith could go to the sheriff to complain. If Turner could hold on a while longer, then the money was his. And if the sheriff would catch Smith during another one of his robberies and put him in jail, then it would be even better.

"I'll try to find him," Gabe said curtly, rising from the chair. At the door, he turned back. "You have no idea where he is hiding?"

"I swear I'd tell you if I had the smallest inkling," Turner answered, taking off his wrinkled coat and placing it on a chair near the bed.

Gabe believed him. It was in Turner's interest to help Gabe catch Smith or whatever his name was. He frowned and absently he noticed a card had fallen face up from the discarded coat, only one card, not a whole deck. His first thought was that the young banker was usually cheating and had hidden the card in his sleeve. He expected this of Turner. He approached the chair and picked up the card from the floor. The queen of spades smiled, almost winked at him.

Gabe turned it in his hands. It was marked. So the

young Turner was cheating. No surprise here.

"There it was," Turner exclaimed extending his hand for the card.

Gabe looked at the card, trying to understand why it was pulling at his memory. It triggered the flash of an image. A man shot dead in a dark alley, saying with his last breath, 'The queen of spades.'

"You killed the card player," he said stepping back and placing the card in his own pocket.

"What? What are you talking about? I know no card player," Turner denied and a muscle under his left eye started to jerk nervously.

"Oh yes, you knew him. The gambler new in town who played cards every night at the saloon. You were there too."

"You don't know this," Turner argued again.

"Yes, I know. I saw you coming out of the millinery and vanishing in the dark alley between the two buildings across the street. A moment later a shot was fired and I found the gambler bleeding in the alley. Before dying, he said 'the queen of spades'. It was the only identification of his killer, because he probably didn't know your name and this was all the proof he had."

"A crazy old man. Any person could have a card, the queen of spades or whatever. This is no proof that the person is guilty," Turner replied, becoming increasingly more agitated. He stole a glance at his gun which was still on the floor where he'd dropped it.

Gabe saw him looking at the gun. "Don't even think of it, unless you have a death wish. I'm much faster with a gun than you."

With another longing look at his gun, Turner abandoned the plan to surprise the deputy and shoot him, admitting that Gabe was probably right and he was much faster than Turner was with a gun. He decided to stick to his own story. "Queen of spades or not, you have no proof."

That was unfortunately true, but Gabe needed to know the truth. "You killed him. The details fit together. You played cards with him earlier that night at the saloon. Then when you saw him in the alley, you shot him. Why?"

Turner raked his hair with his fingers. "It was an accident. I told him he cheated, which was the truth. He was a cheater and a crook. I wanted to prove it to him and I grabbed his arm and searched his sleeve. I found this marked card, the queen of spades. I was enraged, it's true, but the idiot pulled a gun on me. Do you hear me? It was his gun. We wrestled and the gun discharged and he was shot. I panicked and I dropped the gun right there and I ran away," Turner said angry again when he remembered that moment and the terror he experienced when he realized he might have killed the gambler. Next day he calmed down. Nobody knew anything and there was no proof. "It was an accident and you have no proof that I did it. I'll deny everything in front of the judge. Who do you think the judge will believe? Me, an outstanding businessman, well-known despite my recent misunderstanding with my uncle, or you, a stranger in town, arrived only a few months ago, who no one knows or trusts?" He smirked liking this idea.

Gabe had to admit it was all circumstantial and

indeed he had no proof that would stand up in court. Turner was a crook, even a thief, and it could have been an accident as he said. Tired all of a sudden, he had to decide what he could do in this situation. "I appreciate that you told me what happened. It tore at me not to know and understand. If you are on tomorrow's train out of town and never return, I'll forget about it. If you chose to stay, I'll take my chances with the judge. Admit it, Turner, you're finished in this town. Go away." And saying this Gabe left the room.

He went straight to the milliner and entered through the back door. The locked door was no big obstacle for him as he used some of his skills from his tumultuous youth and opened it quickly with the help of his knife and a wire. The house was quiet, the lady milliner deep in sleep upstairs. She didn't need to know the truth. When confronted by Turner the next day she had to be and look genuinely surprised that the portmanteau with the money had vanished.

He took the money and left as quietly as he had entered. He went straight to the old banker's house and woke him up. Without any explanations, he deposited all the money into his care. He knew he could trust old man Turner with it.

When dawn started to light up the sky, Gabe McCarthy collapsed in the chair behind the desk, in the sheriff's office, envying the prisoners in his jail who had a bed. Placing his head on his arms on the desk, he fell asleep.

CHAPTER 23

Like any farmer, Pierce liked to wake up early in the morning, perky and ready to start a work day. He felt quite well, despite a nagging pain in his wounded shoulder. As he was eager to return home, he figured he'd be able to drive the buggy with his right hand only, and let Hero, his horse do the rest of the work. It was better than laying here in the doctor's office and doing nothing, having no idea what was going on at the ranch. It simply drove him crazy. Yes, his shoulder was wounded, but the rest of him was all right.

That said, he ignored the doctor's protests and getting up, he was ready to go home. Finally, the doctor caved in and even confessed that there was a man, sent by rancher Maitland to inquire about his health. He was presently at the stables, but he could send a boy after him. The man could drive Pierce back to the ranch.

It so happened that the man driving Pierce's buggy was Tom Bald Eagle and secretly Pierce was happy to see him and to have company on the road. Tom told him about the round-up of the cattle and sorting which animal belonged to what ranch. They had discovered hidden in the chuck wagon some jewelry and money placed there by the train robber. Tom had already given it to the sheriff's deputy.

They drove talking like that and Pierce feasted his eyes again on the beauty of this land on this warm summer morning.

When the ranch house could be seen in the distance, Tom stopped the buggy, untied his own horse from the back and saluting, rode off across the fields to where his men were taking care of the large herd of cattle.

Pierce had no trouble driving the rest of the way. His horse knew the direction and was also eager to get back home.

An eerie silence welcomed him when he stopped the buggy in front of the barn. Strange. It's true not many people were left here, only Warner and Aunt Edith, but there should be some signs of life nevertheless. He jumped down wincing at his jarred shoulder. He turned toward the house and saw the door opening and Warner stepping on the porch.

"Well, boy," Warner said taking his time to light his smelly cigar that Pierce had started to hate. "Did you think you could defeat me just by getting rid of Luke and the other two? Think again." Warner moved his head slightly, looking beyond Pierce in the general direction of the bunkhouse.

Pierce turned again. The roughest bunch of men that could plague the west was standing there, sneering and jeering in anticipation of an interesting confrontation. The only one not cracking a smile was dressed all in black and by his position in the middle of them, Pierce assumed he was their leader.

Warner nodded with satisfaction. "Just because I feel generous today, I will give you one more chance. Climb back up in that buggy of yours and go as far away as you can and never come back. Otherwise, I'll let these gentlemen deal with you and, just so you know, mercy is not in their vocabulary."

Pierce didn't need to think. "I can't do that,

Warner. You know that. This is my land, this is my life. Without the land, I have no reason to live."

"So be it," Warner said, respecting Pierce's decision and also knowing what was to follow.

"So be it," Pierce echoed, knowing too that he had no chance to fight all five of them. Not like this in an open shoot-out. He looked up at the bright blue Wyoming sky, then across the prairie at this land that he loved, and made peace with himself and his decision and with Bill who had given him this chance. Then he crossed himself thinking that no one would care to bring a pastor to say a few words if he died.

His gesture spurred the men in action. One produced a thick rope and started twirling it threateningly.

"Let's string him from the beam in the barn," shouted another.

A rifle shot in the air tempered down their enthusiasm. Aunt Edith stood on the porch at a distance from Warner. The old Winchester was still smoking from being fired. "There will be no stringing from the barn beam," she said with an authority Pierce didn't know she had.

"Aw, Ma, don't spoil their pleasure," their leader said, somewhat amused.

What was going on here? Pierce looked at her poleaxed. "Ma?" he repeated stricken. "What's going on Aunt Edith?"

Her eyes hardened. "Yes. This is my son. He calls himself Joe Smith now." She pointed at the leader dressed in black. Seeing the questions in Pierce's eyes, she continued almost angry. "No, I didn't know anything. I was told he died in the mining camp and I believed it. I had a surprise when he showed up here yesterday night."

The men hooted with laughter. "She was told you were dead, you heard that, Boss? In a mining camp, no less…" one said.

"Tell us that we can string him from the beam, Boss. You know how it is – if you let him live, he'll come back to bite you. You heard him. He's not going anywhere," another one added.

Without hesitation Aunt Edith fired the rifle one

more time to get their attention. "As I said, there will be no stringing. That doesn't mean it can not be a fair fight. In fact, it is going to be even better. One of you is going to face this farmer boy in a fair gunfight. And I mean fair. I'll make sure it is so," she said and patted her rifle.

"Why, Ma?" Aunt Edith's son asked genuinely curious. Not that he minded. He didn't need any help from his men to kill this untried farmer boy, who, he was sure, had no idea how real men fought in the west.

"Because he gave me shelter when no one would. I figure he deserves a fair chance. If he can't make it, than it's his fault," she answered, her voice strangely wobbly now.

Her son nodded his understanding and he stepped in the middle of the yard, away from the others, facing Pierce. "Are you ready, farmer boy?"

"To meet your Maker," another man filled in and they all laughed, now excited by the idea of a gunfight.

The talk didn't bother Pierce. An unusual calm came over him. No excitement, no fear, no nerves. Exactly as Gabe McCarthy had taught him, he concentrated only on his opponent's eyes and especially on his hand. Nothing else mattered. He saw his fingers jerking and in a reflexive gesture Pierce's gun was out and firing.

The other one was a fraction of a second behind. He was hit in his leg and with a cry of pain, he dropped the gun and grabbed his thigh, falling to the ground.

"Ma, kill him," he shouted just as Pierce fired again into the dropped gun moving it a yard away from the wounded man.

His men were stunned by this turn of events. Never had they imagined that their boss, whose gun fighting skills were legendary, would be shot by a farmer boy, young and without experience.

The gunfighter rolled his wounded body closer to the gun and grabbing it, turned toward Pierce. A shot rang out and he fell face up.

From behind the barn, John Gorman and four of his men rode in the yard. In the excitement and noise of the fight, no one heard them approaching. Gorman blew his still smoking gun and placed it back in his holster.

Warner ignored them. "Darn Edith, you knew the boy was faster," he muttered still puffing his cigar.

She was not on the porch any longer. Only her discarded rifle lay there. Warner considered grabbing it for a moment. But what to do with it? It was clear that the farmer boy had won. Helped by neighbors like Gorman or not, the boy had proven himself a worthy adversary.

Pierce holstered his own gun. The fight was over. He extended his hand to John Gorman. "Thank you for your timely arrival and help." He knew he could have shot his opponent himself, but perhaps it was better this way, he thought, looking at Aunt Edith. She was sitting on the ground, heedless of all the dust, holding her son's head in her lap and touching gently his face and his hair.

Gorman shook Pierce's hand. "You're welcome. What are neighbors for? To help each other when in need. Tom Bald Eagle alerted me of your predicament and of this new danger you were facing."

Gorman's men were tying the hands of the other outlaws, preparing a wagon to take them to town.

Perhaps they might have put up a fight, but they were dazed by everything that had happened, their invincible leader dead so unexpectedly and they surrounded by angry, determined men.

"I'll take them to town," Gorman said. "The dead one included. Tom told me you're not entirely healed."

Aunt Edith raised her head. "Mr. Gorman, please see that he has a nice burial. I'll pay for it. Tell the undertaker to let me know when and where and I'll be there," she said with dignity, trying to hide her obvious grief and not quite succeeding. "His name was Jacob Heller and he was thirty-two years of age," she added.

"Consider it done, ma'am," Gorman replied politely. Then he looked around, where his men had the situation well in hand and his eyes stopped at Warner, who was puffing his cigar, what else? His face was inscrutable as usual.

Anticipating his question, Pierce said, "No. I'll take care of him."

Gorman frowned. "Are you sure? I would gladly relieve you of the burden of having to see him one more day."

"Very sure, thank you. I'll deal with him myself," Pierce answered.

The wagon with the tied up robbers was on its way to town to the Sheriff's Office and jail, and Gorman followed them to make sure there would not be any mishap on the road.

Aunt Edith, looking aged and grieving, climbed the steps slowly and entered the house. Pierce stopped on the porch and looked back at the yard.

"Well boy, you decided that you need me and my advice after all," Warner said.

Pierce looked at him and shook his head. He was amazed by the shrewdness and cunning of the older man. Wasn't Warner quite the survivor? "No, I don't," Pierce said finally. "Just so you know, I would take you to jail in a heartbeat."

"Why don't you?"

"I promised Vanessa not to hurt you. Admit it Warner, your time here is at an end. I'll take you to the train tomorrow. I don't care where you go, east or west, as long as it's far away from here. I'll make sure that when the train leaves, you're on it."

"What about Edith? She was Joe Smith's, or whatever his name was, mother. Are you going to take her to the train too?"

"Of course not. She is my Aunt Edith and she'd done nothing wrong or harmful in her life. She knew nothing. Now she's part of my family. Her home is here with me."

CHAPTER 24

Warner didn't give Pierce any trouble over leaving and neither did he try to delay their departure. Early in the morning, he was ready with a large trunk and a portmanteau waiting on the porch. Pierce didn't care what he'd packed in there, as long as he was leaving.

Warner didn't look back, didn't make conversation on the way to town, and didn't try one more time to convince Pierce to let him stay. It was not that his fighting spirit went out of him. No, not at all. He was alert as always and his eyes lively. He was probably cutting his losses short and plotting his next move.

As he'd promised, Pierce waited until he saw the train carrying Warner away. To his surprise, the older man chose to go east to St. Louis. Pierce didn't comment or asked what Warner's plans were. It was not his business and he was not interested to know. He was just happy to see him go.

Besides, he had a busy morning ahead and was more concerned about how his own plans would succeed than about Warner's fate.

Pierce looked after the train gaining speed and becoming smaller and smaller in the distance. He waved at Timmy, the train station clerk, and jumping back in his buggy, drove to his first stop of the day, the Sheriff's Office.

To his surprise, he found Gabe McCarthy outside, on the small bench in front of the window, stretching his long legs in front of him, with his hat low almost covering his face. "Hey, Gabe what are you doing here?"

The deputy measured him up and down lazily. "Well, kid, since you moved here, the jail is filling up steadily. You'd think we are holding a social event of the outlaws. They are so many that the jail is bursting at the seams."

Pierce looked at him, not sure if his friend was joking or if he was serious. "I'm sorry. That's why you're sitting outside?"

Now Gabe laughed. "No, kid. I'm watching for two marshals to take at least some of the outlaws to the Territorial Prison. By the way, your brother came back last night, hauling with him another bunch of outlaws."

Pierce's eyes lit up at the news. "Bill is here? That's great. I have to talk to him." And he opened the door to the office.

"Wait. He's not alone," Gabe said. It was too late to stop him, as Pierce had already entered the front room.

Inside the office, only too late Pierce saw amazed that his brother Bill, the severe sheriff all outlaws feared, had his arms around an elegant brunette lady and was kissing her with all his might.

"I told you to wait outside," Bill barked, reluctantly separating his lips from the lady's, but continuing to keep his arms around her. He turned his head and saw Pierce. "Oh, it's you, kid."

The brunette looked Pierce over with curiosity. "Who are you?" she asked.

Pierce took off his hat embarrassed. "I'm the younger brother. Pierce Monroe is my name, ma'am."

She laughed, a pleasant sound like tiny bells. "Call me, Francine. We are soon to be related."

"She is my affianced bride," Bill announced,

looking at her with pride.

This surprised Pierce. He couldn't imagine how his brother, a rough and tough western sheriff could have earned the heart of this elegant and sophisticated eastern lady. For a moment, he wondered how it would be to have such a lady of quality look at him with the same love that Francine showed to his brother, Bill.

Then he shook himself. Nah, it wouldn't work. He couldn't see Francine smiling while washing laundry in the copper tub outside or weeding their vegetable garden. He needed a strong woman unafraid to share with him the hard life on a ranch. He needed... Amy Poole. That's who he needed and he'd better hurry along to convince her to marry him.

Meanwhile, Bill, continuing to hold on to Francine, like afraid she might go away if he didn't, rummaged with the other hand inside the top drawer of his desk. Finding what he was looking for, he handed Pierce some papers.

"What is this?" Pierce asked glancing over the papers. His eyes widened and he read them with more attention. One was the deed to the ranch, the whole ranch, and the second was a quitclaim deed, transferring the ranch, all of it, into Pierce's name.

"Aside from the fact that my jail is full with a lot of miscreants you caught, John Gorman visited me this morning. It seems that the news of your exploits have spread all over the county. Take it. You deserve it. The ranch is yours."

Pierce was speechless. He needed to pinch himself to be sure he was not dreaming. "The deal was only for half the ranch," he managed to observe weakly.

"What would I do with the other half?" Bill's voice boomed. "I'm a sheriff and I like living in town. Francine is used to living in big city Baltimore. She likes Laramie, but I can't ask her to live in the unavoidable isolation of a ranch."

"I thank you, but in all honesty you should know that I couldn't have succeeded without the help of John Gorman and Elliott Maitland. I didn't exactly do it on my own, alone," Pierce mentioned, because he had to tell Bill the truth.

"Well, of course, they helped you. This is how we survive, neighbors help each other. No one lives entirely alone. Now please take your papers and go keep Gabe company outside. I still have some talking to do with Francine."

Pierce smiled, placed the papers inside his shirt and raising his hand said another Thank you and turned to go.

Bill's voice, a bit more gentle this time, stopped him in the doorway. "You did great, Pierce. I'm proud of you. Now go."

For some idiotic reason Pierce couldn't understand, tears pooled at the corners of his eyes after this conversation with his brother. He pulled the door shut after him.

"Well, kid, how did the meeting go?" Gabe asked him, patting the empty place near him on the bench.

"Pretty good. I can't complain," Pierce answered still thinking and feeling warm at his brother's words. "Gabe, I want to tell you something. I was lucky and my neighbors are good men and helped me. But it was you who guided and watched over me all along."

"Nah, you don't have to feel obliged..."

"I don't. Simply, because you are my friend. I have good neighbors and a brother I admire, but you are special to me. You are my friend," Pierce repeated. "And now I have a stubborn woman to convince to marry me."

"You too? Is this a contagious disease in town?" Gabe asked gruffly, trying to hide the deep emotion Pierce's words caused him.

Whistling, Pierce turned the buggy around and drove to the milliner's shop.

He entered the shop and pulled his hat off, intimidated as always when he entered in such an exclusive women's world, full of flowers and feathers, silk and gauze, and other delicate and colorful fabrics smelling of perfume.

Would Amy be willing to leave this world for the life of hard work on the ranch that he offered her?

He found inside only the shop owner arranging a bold confection on a display head. "Excuse me, I'd like to talk to Amy."

THE YOUNGER BROTHER

The shopkeeper turned to face him and Pierce saw that she was upset. "Amy left me. I offered to share my room with her and she left me. What is the matter with the world, I ask you? They all leave me. They hurl awful accusations at me and then leave. Not Amy, I'm talking about... Never mind." She sniffed and turned back to her arrangement.

Pierce hopped from one foot to the other. Amy left? When she said making hats was the dream of her life? "Excuse me, do you know where she went?"

She waved her hand vaguely. "Oh, he said he's going where the train will carry him."

"Amy. I'm talking about Amy," Pierce corrected her with impatience.

"Oh, Amy went back to the saloon."

To the saloon? What on earth made Amy return to that place? Pierce left the millinery and turning the buggy around again, drove fast to Tom Wilkes' saloon. It was mid-day and the locale was rather empty, except for two cowboys talking heatedly about some horse with a bottle of whiskey on the table between them. At the bar, the owner was propping his face in his palm, masking a yawn with the other.

"Excuse me, I'm looking for the young boy who cleaned here," Pierce asked him.

The saloonkeeper measured him with a knowing look. "He quit a few days ago and I haven't seen him since. I guess he found a better patron. You're too late," he added sneering.

Before Pierce understood the innuendo, he was approached by one of the saloon girls who had just come from upstairs. "Come," she said, and steering him toward the stairs, she murmured for his ears only, "I know who you are. Amy is upstairs. I'll take you to her."

She guided him along a narrow hallway to one of the rooms. She opened the door and pushed him inside, closing the door.

There, in the middle of four saloon girls amused, was his sweet Amy singing and waving a hand with a glass full of whiskey in her hand. She looked at him and smiled, "Priece, Priss…" she frowned and tried again. "Price, no…ah,…you came for me," she exclaimed happily and fell with her face on the table covered with red velvet, dropping the glass on the carpeted floor.

"Amy!" Pierce cried, lifting Amy from the table. His bride was drunk and snoring softly. "What did you do to her?" he asked, although it was pretty obvious what.

The girls giggled amused, not the fake laughter meant to attract the saloon customers.

"Amy came to say Good-bye to us," one of them explained.

"She said she decided to get married to a rancher called Pierce Monroe, younger brother of the sheriff," another filled in.

"The sheriff - now that is one attractive man," the third one said dreamily.

"Sorry to disappoint, ladies, but the sheriff is getting married too," Pierce said carrying his future bride out of the room, followed by a choir of disappointed sighs.

The girl who had brought him in, guided him to the side stairs outside. "You treat her well, you hear?"

she said after him.

When he reached his buggy and with a last effort placed Amy up on the seat, drops of blood were noticeable on his shirt and his shoulder started throbbing. But he was happy that he found his bride. He climbed up on the seat and gathered Amy to him. Then he drove away. Home, to his ranch.

CHAPTER 25

Pierce Monroe and Amy Poole were married the next Sunday by the pastor at the Methodist Episcopal Church. The church had been built thirty years earlier in 1869 on the east side of 2nd Street, one of the oldest church buildings in Wyoming. Because they were both quite alone in the world and of modest means, they didn't plan a big wedding. Pierce asked his friend Gabe McCarthy to stand up with him and Amy invited Miss Priscilla, who had been so generous and willing to help her.

Aunt Edith promised to cook enough food for whatever guests they were having. Not many, Pierce advised her, maybe no one would come at the ranch house to celebrate with them. Both he and Amy were rather new in town and not many people knew them. Pierce didn't think his brother Bill would have time to come or cared enough to do it, although he'd been invited.

Not only Bill did come to church and sat in the

front pew near Aunt Edith, but his affianced bride, Francine surprised them and gifted Amy with a pretty, elegant blue dress – it was too late to order a wedding gown and this was the best she could find at the dressmaker's shop in town. Amy was very happy, because she really wanted to look pretty on this special day.

Their neighbors, John Gorman and Elliott Maitland both came to church and so did many of their men. Some people in town, who came to worship that morning stayed for the wedding too. And so, Pierce and Amy had a lot more attendance than they bargained for and many came to the ranch to celebrate. As one cheeky cowboy observed, a wedding is always an opportunity to have fun and spend time with one's neighbors.

Pierce and Amy lived happily a long life together, despite natural difficulties and moments of sorrow, like losing a daughter in infancy to scarlet fever. The ranch was prosperous due to their hard work and determination, overcoming years of drought and blizzards that killed some of their cattle.

THE YOUNGER BROTHER

Aunt Edith was considered as one of the family, helping not only by cooking, but also helping Amy to raise her six living children, four boys and two girls.

The sheriff married his beloved Francine and he built her a Victorian house in town that rivaled the famous Ivinson Mansion. They had no children, but Pierce's youngest girl came to live with them later in life and one of his sons followed Bill in his steps by becoming sheriff in Laramie. That happened much later on, though.

As for two other characters in this story, John Gorman continued to mourn the loss of his intended, Esme, and told everyone in town he never wanted to marry, until love took him by storm and left him dazzled.

What about Gabe McCarthy? - you'd ask. Gabe, who was always a wanderer, moving on before becoming too attached to a place, discovered that it was not so easy to leave this town. He thought he was a stranger in town as always, but he found out that the friendly people in Laramie didn't consider him so.

This is another tale of the Old Wyoming better

left for another time.

* * *

Historical Note – Located on Ivinson Street, Kuster Hotel was built in 1869, by the Dawson brothers costing $5,000 at the time. It is the oldest stone building in Laramie. At the beginning it served as a hotel for traveling cowboys and railroad workers and also as a depot for the Fort Collins and Walden stage line, and later on as a bus depot. The hotel had twenty-six rooms and a restaurant on the first floor. The original building had larger windows with cornices and lintels over them, and arches over the entrance. These architectural details have been lost to later remodeling, in late 1920s, when simpler lines were preferred for the front of the building.

* * *

If you enjoyed reading this book, please leave a brief review on Amazon. I welcome all your comments and suggestions.

Keep reading for an exclusive sneak peek of *A Stranger In Town*, Book 2 of the *Tales Of Old Wyoming* series.

VIVIAN SINCLAIR

A Stranger In

Town

VIVIAN SINCLAIR

CHAPTER 1

Dry Creek, Texas, 1878

It was a dusty small town, a speck on the map, somewhere north of Fort Worth, near the Texas-Oklahoma border. It was near sunset, and in one of the three saloons in town the piano played a lively tune and the customers saw to their business as they did every evening. Three tables were occupied by the usual card players. At the bar several cowboys were drinking whiskey and lamenting the lack of rain that dried all the grass and of course, the creek. The girls were lazily walking from one customer to the other trying their best to convince some younger naïve cowboy to buy them a drink.

The relative peaceful evening was interrupted when the swinging doors were pushed open and a man dressed in dark clothes and wearing a long duster, entered the saloon, stopping right there, near the entrance.

A STRANGER IN TOWN

He studied the people present in the hall, and nodded satisfied. His eyes focused on a man in his thirties, drinking whiskey at the bar.

"Gabe McCarthy, I've been following you from Amarillo. You have the reputation of being the fastest draw. Let's see how fast you are." He pulled aside his duster revealing his low buckled holster. A challenge had been issued.

The man at the bar blinked and trying to maintain his composure said, "I don't know you and I'm not fighting with you."

"You, with your red bandanna, you are a coward as I expected," the gunslinger proclaimed emphatically. It was more than a challenge, it was a grave insult and by the laws of the west the challenged man had to answer.

"I'm no coward," the man at the bar said and reached for his gun.

He had his hand on it, when the challenger draw lightning fast and fired.

A stunned silence reigned in the saloon.

The newcomer looked at the prone body on the

floor, and at his still smoking gun. He placed it back in his holster. "My name is Joe Brewster. Remember it. I'm the fastest gun in all Texas."

One of the card players at a table on his right, stood up slowly. "You killed an innocent man for nothing, Joe Brewster. I was hoping you'll go away without a gunfight. I'm the one you're looking for. I'm Gabe McCarthy."

The other players left the table immediately and the customers stayed away from the direct path between the two confronting men. But nobody left the saloon, all eager to see what would happen.

The sardonic smile froze on the gunslinger's face. He looked from the body on the floor to the one standing near the table. "You can't be."

"I sure am. You see I don't always wear a red bandanna." He opened his coat and pulled out a red neckerchief. "Only sometimes." He placed it back in his pocket without mentioning that it was all he had left from his mother and he carried it with him always.

The gunslinger's eyes twitched and without

warning he reached for his gun. What happened next, nobody could say. The people present in the saloon swore that they didn't see the gambler drawing. Yet, somehow the gun was in his hand and the gunslinger fell to the floor.

"I saw it mister," a man with a sheriff's star pinned on his shirt told him. "He came here with the purpose to kill you. We all saw. You fired in self defense."

"Yeah," echoed another. "Sam, here, was a good man. His family will have at least the comfort that his killer is dead and he is avenged."

What comfort could this be, when the family lost their dear one? - the gambler wondered, tired to be in this situation, to avoid killers again and again.

He sighed and suddenly needed to breathe fresh air. When he was at the door he heard a younger cowboy calling him. "Hey mister, you forgot your winnings."

"Leave it for the funeral of the innocent man caught in a fight that was not his own," the gambler said, his hand on the swinging door. He left without looking back.

* * *

To find out about new releases and about other books written by Vivian Sinclair visit her website at VivianSinclairBooks.com or follow her on the Author page at Amazon, Facebook at Vivian Sinclair Books, or on GoodReads.com

Old West Wyoming - western historical fiction
Book 1 - A Western Christmas
Book 2 - The Train To Laramie
Book 3 - The Last Stagecoach

Tales Of Old Wyoming – western historical fiction
Book 1 – The Younger Brother
Book 2 – A Stranger In Town
Book 3 – Going West
Book 4 – The Revenge

Starting Over in Wyoming - western contemporary fiction
Book 1 – Riding Alone
Book 2 – The Old Homestead
Book 3 – On The Hunt

Maitland Legacy, A Family Saga - western contemporary fiction
Book 1 – Lost In Wyoming – Lance's story
Book 2 – Moon Over Laramie – Tristan's story

A STRANGER IN TOWN

Book 3 – Christmas In Cheyenne – Raul's story

Wyoming Christmas – western contemporary fiction
Book 1 – Footprints In The Snow – Tom's story
Book 2 – A Visitor For Christmas – Brianna's story
Book 3 – Trapped On The Mountain – Chris' story

Summer Days In Wyoming - western contemporary fiction
Book 1 – A Ride In The Afternoon
Book 2 – Fire At Midnight
Book 3 – Misty Meadows At Dawn

Tales of Old Wyoming - western historical fiction
Book 1 – A Stranger In Town
Book 2 – Going West
Book 3 – The Younger Brother

Seattle Rain series - women's fiction novels
Book 1 - A Walk In The Rain
Book 2 – Rain, Again!
Book 3 – After The Rain

Virginia Lovers - contemporary romance:
Book 1 – Alexandra's Garden
Book 2 – Ariel's Summer Vacation
Book 3 – Lulu's Christmas Wish

A Guest At The Ranch – western contemporary romance

Storm In A Glass Of Water – a small town story

23991134R00162

Made in the USA
San Bernardino, CA
01 February 2019